ENCHANTED JOURNEYS

An anthology of extracts from Ireland's best
modern writers for children

ROBERT DUNBAR

Robert Dunbar is a lecturer in the Church of Ireland College of Education. He also teaches a course in children's literature at Trinity College Dublin, and organises and teaches on the TCD course leading to the Diploma in Children's Literature. He is a regular reviewer of children's books for a wide range of newspapers, magazines and radio programmes. He was born in Ballymoney, Co. Antrim, and now lives in Dublin.

ENCHANTED JOURNEYS

EDITED BY
ROBERT DUNBAR

Illustrated by Aileen Johnston

THE O'BRIEN PRESS
DUBLIN

IRISH AMERICAN BOOK COMPANY (IABC)
Boulder, Colorado

First published 1997 by The O'Brien Press Ltd.
20 Victoria Road, Rathgar, Dublin 6, Ireland.
Tel. +353 1 4923333; Fax. +353 1 4922777
e-mail: books@obrien.ie
website: http://www.obrien.ie

Published in the USA by the
Irish American Book Company (IABC)
6309 Monarch Park Place, Suite 101,
Niwot, Colorado 80503
Office: Tel. 303-652-2710 Fax. 303-652-2689
Orders: Tel. 800-452-7115 Fax. 800-401-9705

ISBN: 0-86278-518-9

British Library Cataloguing-in-publication Data
A catalogue reference for this book is available
from the British Library

1 2 3 4 5 6 7 8 9 10
97 98 99 00 01 02 03 04 05

The O'Brien Press receives assistance from
The Arts Council/An Chomhairle Ealaíon

Typesetting, layout, design: The O'Brien Press Ltd.
Cover illustration: Aileen Johnston
Cover separations: Lithoset Ltd., Dublin
Printing: MPG Books Ltd.

Contents

DEDICATION

For Carole, Dominic and Gráinne,
with whom most of my enchanted journeys
have been shared

INTRODUCTION

All good stories for children offer the prospect of 'enchanted journeys', the opportunity for young readers to embark imaginatively on voyages of discovery. When these stories are drawn from the riches of Irish writing for children, the voyages assume a fascinating character of their own. This uniqueness, which this anthology celebrates, derives from a blend of factors, among which the country's geography, its history and its long association with oral and written narrative are of key significance. The seventeen extracts which comprise the anthology are so arranged as to take the reader on a journey backwards through time from the present day to the early 1940s, providing some insights into the origins and development of what is now, in the late 1990s, usually referred to as 'modern Irish children's literature', while demonstrating the continuing significance of the factors mentioned earlier. In the main, the selection has been made with readers aged ten to twelve in mind, a recognition of the fact that it is for this age group that most Irish children's literature has, until very recently, been primarily intended. Older readers should, however, find much here to interest them also.

The fifty or so years reviewed in this anthology have seen remarkable social, economic and political development in Ireland. Its sense of self and the perception of it by the wider world have both undergone considerable transformation. In a metaphorical sense,

its place in that world has changed. But what, obviously, has not changed is its geographical condition of being an island, a condition which has influenced the nature of much of the writing – whether for adults or children – which has emanated from it. Where Irish children's literature is concerned, the appeal of an island setting has always been strong, understandably so, given the possibility of thrilling adventure on the seas around an often treacherous coastline and the opportunity for narratives where the young, in isolated locations, can find and be themselves. Add to these attractions a history which can itself be seen in terms of a narrative composed of journeys to and from an island, and we have the starting points for numerous stories of exploration and survival.

In the earlier and less enduring examples of the genre the emphasis tends to be on the adventure itself; as the genre develops, this gives way to deeper and more sensitive characterisation and to a more powerful and more resonant evocation of place. Even in the fifteen years which separate Conor O'Brien's *The Runaways* (1941) and Eilís Dillon's *The Island of Horses* (1956) such a development is visible. In the former, three English boys find themselves on Croaghmore, forced to share temporary accommodation with an Irishman on the run: but the principal concern is less with the politics than with the boys' determination to involve 'the refugee' in their own projected expedition to Skye. Pat and Danny, the boys in *The Island of Horses*, may be younger than O'Brien's, but they are given a capacity to respond to (and reflect on) the natural world which O'Brien's lads are denied. Their island, however, remains a place apart – 'with nothing between it and America' – though it is a place very firmly given its own reality, one which credibly instils in the boys their sense of 'a terrible, primitive fear'.

From islands somewhere off the coast of Ireland in O'Brien and Dillon we move, with the Patricia Lynch and Walter Macken excerpts, to the larger island itself and in both cases to an Ireland to which the traveller returns. But which Ireland is it? When Timothy Driscoll comes back to his family's warm welcome in Lynch's *The Old Black Sea Chest* (1958) the reader's attention is drawn to 'the coloured parchment map of Ireland in ancient times' which hangs on the wall. Young Milo Driscoll notes it too and reflects: 'How different it was from the new shining map beside the big window at school. He liked this old one best, but he knew the new map was supposed to be more correct.' It is a homecoming which, as the startling disclosure at the end of the extract reveals, is to be more problematic than it initially appears. Similarly, for Finn and Derval in Macken's *Flight of the Doves* (1968) the prelude to their return to Ireland is to be filled with apprehension and uncertainty. The only comfort Derval allows himself on the journey is a school text – 'a geography book with coloured maps of all the countries of the world in it' – but its value is idealistic rather than practical.

The 'idealistic' and the 'practical' are the dualities with which Irish children's historical fiction generally deals, a consequence of its concentration on flashpoint periods when conflicting ideologies meet and when conflicting loyalties are tested. The backwards journey to these periods in children's historical fiction involves conveying to the young what few of them will have: a sense of history. This is something more complex than the factual knowledge obtainable in the traditional textbook, since it demands an imaginative identification with a time, setting and characters well removed from a child's reality. Even where a particular event has become part of the national consciousness, the novelist has to move beneath the facts and figures to resurrect the women, men and children whose lives have been largely buried in the abstraction known as 'history'.

The excerpts in this anthology from Irish children's historical fiction admirably perform this act of resurrection and in the process chart their own 'enchanted journeys'. Meta Mayne Reid's 1969 novel *The Two Rebels* has its factual origin in the Antrim town uprising of 1798. The history, however, is presented more as an offstage event, since the book is primarily concerned with the adventures of two of the participants in the struggle, one of poor Presbyterian farming stock, the other an aristocrat in the Protestant liberal mould. From the moment in the Prologue to the novel when twelve-year-old twins Andrew and Bess McIlroy overhear their uncle and his friend rehearse the credo of the United Irishmen brotherhood, its rhythms remain a sort of mesmeric talisman, making them ready converts to the cause. The excerpt here is a journey towards an understanding of those factors which have helped to make contemporary Ulster what it is, particularly towards an understanding of the shifts in loyalties which there have been since 1798.

There is similar illumination of the manner in which historical events continue to cast a long shadow in Tom McCaughren's *In Search of the Liberty Tree* (1994). This is a further contribution to our understanding of the events of 1798 in, as with Meta Mayne Reid, an Ulster setting. Through the eyes of two young friends, Joshua Watson and Sammy Johnston, we are given glimpses of an adult world divided in its loyalties and passionately violent in defence of them. It is part of the novelist's skill here to involve the two boys in events in a way which is totally convincing. As they watch the assembling of the English soldiery Joshua perceives a link between the red of their tunics and the colour of blood, a moment paralleled later when Sammy's house is raided and he and his father are removed by the same bayonet-wielding militiamen.

Just over a century later, in Siobhán Parkinson's *Amelia* (1993), the securities of middle-class Dublin life are being threatened by the winds of social and political change. Parkinson, in her portrayal of a young girl excitedly preparing for her birthday party, captures a way of life which, for all its outward confidence, is essentially shaky and fragile. Even a shopping expedition, where the details of the purchases are carefully enumerated, involves Mama telling a fib; even a mended orangery roof, a sparkling new dress and promises of motorcar rides cannot prevent an 'anxious glance' between the parents. The destinies of the various individuals engage our attention and win our sympathy. But the sense of time's inexorable movement strikes us just as poignantly.

Precisely the same comments are applicable – though the period and setting could hardly be more different from Parkinson's to Sam McBratney's *The Chieftain's Daughter* (1993), where the novel's themes assume an almost mythic dimension: friendship and enmity, passion and hatred, trust and betrayal, all reconstructed in the tale of an Ireland of fifteen centuries ago, related by the ancient chief Dinn Keane. At the heart of the story lies an unforgettable evocation of young love kindled and young love killed, a tragedy numbing in its unfolding. The deceptively simple language cloaks a narrative technique which, in teasingly moving from past to present, from first person to third, enforces the reader's continuous adjustment of perspective.

The way in which personal and historical change of circumstances can affect everyday lives provides the starting point for Elizabeth O'Hara's *The Hiring Fair* (1993). The unexpected death by drowning of their father means that Sally and Katie Gallagher, aged thirteen and eleven respectively, are forced to become hired servants and, in the process, to leave their Donegal homestead on a journey to the unknown farmyards of Co. Tyrone. O'Hara's graphic and detailed account of the events of the 'hiring day' in Milford and her insights into the interplay between adult and child, buyer and bought, endow her fiction with a feel of documentary realism. Most telling of all, perhaps, is the portrayal of the girls' mother, caught between the urgency to ensure that her children find employment and her anxiety that they do so only on terms which will keep her sense of loss to a minimum. As we leave her at the end of the excerpt the astute bargainer has given way to the grieving parent, who now 'felt even sadder than she had when Jack had drowned'.

For Ellie McLoughlin, the young heroine of Maeve Friel's *Distant Voices* (1994), Donegal serves as point of arrival rather than point of departure. It is there she will travel from her native Derry city to carry out the promise of the words of 'the tall boy-man', Harald Olafsson, who comes to disturb her dreams: 'Only you,' he tells her, 'will know where to find me.' The story of her quest, moving between the real world of her own time and the Viking period of over one thousand years earlier, provides Friel with the opportunity for a time-slip narrative which is handled with stylish assurance. The familiar Derry landscape seems to 'shrink', the modern city vanishes and yet, within a few moments, the Guildhall clock will be ringing and the Army helicopter will set off on its morning patrol. What is dream and what is reality? Like Ellie at the end of the excerpt, the reader is 'possessed', totally engrossed by the prospect of the beckoning journey through time.

When Toss Byrne whispers to the horse Glengarry of 'times past, times present and times to come' in Marita Conlon-McKenna's *Fields of Home* (1996) he describes perfectly the range of possibilities inherent in successful historical fiction. Conlon-McKenna herself, in the magical and incantatory excerpt from the novel with which this anthology opens, matches this aspiration with a piece of writing which, while beautifully controlled and economical, is powerfully suggestive. The 'gift of whispering', handed down from one generation to the next, becomes (rather like the United Irishmen's catechism in *The Two Rebels*) a sort of curative charm, one which will here stand Michael in good stead in whatever new circumstances he will now, post his Famine experiences, encounter: it symbolises the life and energy coursing through young limbs.

From Conlon-McKenna's rural Ireland of the past we move, in Eugene McCabe's *Cyril: The Quest of an Orphaned Squirrel* (1986), John Quinn's *The Summer of Lily and Esme* (1991) and Frank Murphy's *Lockie and Dadge* (1995), to its contemporary equivalent. Changed in detail though the landscape may be, it is still perceived in these novels, though to varying degrees, as a terrain where the individual (or group of individuals) is faced by the need, as McCabe's Cyril expresses it, 'to have someone who could explain things'. While *Cyril* is set exclusively in the natural world, the events described in it have their human (and political) application: the young squirrel, left an orphan, taunted by crows and witness of what seems to be their mindless savagery, feels that the coming lonely winter will be an unbearable threat unless his old friend, Charlie the badger, has some comforting wisdom to offer. The need to find this solace provides the starting point for the search for meaning and understanding which gives the story its structure and theme; and it is this quest which involves Cyril in coming to accept those who are very different from himself.

In the Murphy novel young Lockie is befriended by the mysterious adult known, for reasons he lovingly explains, as 'Dadge'. The boy's gradual acceptance of his new environment and companions does not quite obliterate nagging doubts about future developments or lessen his desire to know who he really is. In Quinn's story Alan McKay is also faced with a new environment and, additionally, with various family tensions and his own loneliness. Interestingly, it is adults here also, in the form of two remarkable old ladies, who take Alan's mind off its own concerns and, in so doing, lead him (and the reader) on a journey into an appreciation of the complex depths of human relationships, a domain where age would seem to be an irrelevant consideration.

While most Irish writers of children's fiction are drawn to an Irish setting (past or present, real or fantasy), an increasing number commendably choose to journey to places beyond their own. Three examples of such writers are included here. In Janet McNeill's *We Three Kings* (1974), an English seaside resort serves as background for a story in which 'the whole history and language and pattern of a family' have been wiped out. It is the task of Dan, the son of the family, to restore it to its previous harmony. Little Obie, in Martin Waddell's *Little Obie and the Flood* (1991), also has a mission of restoration: to ease Marty out of the introspection and lethargy which have dogged her since her father's death and to ensure her gradual integration into her new extended family. Matthew Sweeney's *The Snow Vulture* (1992) focuses on the sibling rivalry of twins Clive and Carl, the rivalry given vivid expression in the contrasting bear and vulture which they respectively fashion out of snow. When their creations frighteningly assume lives of their own and become the embodiments of good and evil, the story develops into a chilling study of the darker side of childhood. All three of these novels place their child protagonists in domestic situations where they must come to terms with others, particularly adults, around them: the games played here tend to be serious and as psychologically testing as cliff-climbing and yacht-sailing.

Here, then, are seventeen 'journeys' chosen from some fifty years of Irish writing for children. They are linked by their Irishness and by their writers' skill in investing them with an enchantment which ensures their enjoyment by readers well beyond the shores of the small island where their creators were born.

Robert Dunbar
Dublin 1997

Marita Conlon-McKenna

from

FIELDS OF HOME

Michael patted Morning Boy's silky coat. The large burn on his side had started to heal, the skin and hair finally knitting together. Glengarry was busy grazing, her long neck bent, her jaws chomping on the blades of grass. One hoof was held at an awkward angle, not supporting her properly. Both horses were still recovering from the fire. All the other horses had gone at this stage, sold off to the highest bidders, a few going to England.

Young Brendan had been offered a job with Mr Delahunt. 'I'll still see some of our horses, Michael,' he said. 'Won't that be grand?'

Michael had to suppress a pang of jealousy as he saw the younger lad's eager and excited face.

Toss Byrne had come down to the stables as the horses were being sold off, moving among the burnt-out buildings. He gave Michael a horse-blanket, two worn bridles and two full sets of harness. Toss said goodbye to the horses in his own fashion. Michael watched the way he went up to each one of them, right up close, his head and lips almost touching their pointed ears, talking to them, whispering to them.

Michael watched as the old man walked towards Glengarry, his voice slow and soothing, getting her to lift her head and listen to him.

'Michael!' He beckoned, and Michael swung himself up over the wooden fence into the paddock.

Toss was whispering away in a low voice to the horse.

'Michael, stand beside me! Listen to me!' ordered Toss. Michael came nearer. 'Michael, you already have the gift of handling horses,' said Toss. 'You like them and care about them and they know and feel it. They trust you because you treat them like intelligent animals, recognising that they get sad and nervous, and angry and scared, and happy and giddy, just like we humans do.'

'Aye!' agreed Michael.

'Michael, you know I have no children, no sons. Today I want to give you a gift – well, much of it you already have. This was passed from my father to me. He got it from his father before him. Move right up close by me.' Michael stood beside the horse, his hand stroking her side. 'Just listen!'

Toss began to whisper and Michael could make out the horse's name, Glengarry. Toss whispered of wind in the trees and green grass growing, of soft rain that fell, and night sky that drew in and stars that watched from above. He spoke of horses that pulled and ploughed and helped man to till the earth that God gave them. He told of horses that carried men into battle in the names of kings and queens, of all the animal kingdom large and small, and of the horse's place as a friend of man.

Glengarry stood totally still, listening, ears pricked, eyes wide and alert as the whispering went on. Toss spoke of times past, times present and times to come. He spoke of the races she'd run, the foals she'd had and would have, and the races they too would run.

Michael barely dared to breathe. Toss whispered to Glengarry of the life-blood that coursed through her body, the energy that must travel to heal her damaged leg and hoof. She seemed to whinny softly, blowing air down her velvety nostrils. Her heart seemed to beat strong and steady as the voice talked on and on to her.

As Michael listened the words changed. They did not seem like normal words, but ran together – it wasn't Gaelic or English or French. But he could sort of understand it, just the way Glengarry seemed to.

Then Toss's voice trailed off. Glengarry sniffed at the man's head and hair, and Toss patted her playfully.

'Aye! She's a good one, Michael, a right good one,' said the older man as they walked back across the field.

'Thank you, Toss!' said Michael. 'I've never heard the gift of whispering before, it's a rare thing.'

'Now you must try it. It'll help you with the horses in future, Michael, mark my words. Call Morning Boy!'

The young horse loved attention and cantered over immediately. Michael was nervous as he bent towards Morning Boy's neck. 'Morning Boy, born as the moon dipped and the sun rose warm from earth ...' whispered Michael.

* * *

It was only a few days' walk to Eily's home. Michael took it good and easy with the horses. Glengarry's leg was improving, but she was still fairly lame.

Walking through the open countryside reminded Michael of the time before when, hungry and scared, dressed in rags and starving, he had walked – walked because his very life had depended on it – with his sisters, Eily and Peggy, at the height of the Great Famine.

He gave a sigh of relief when he finally reached the townland where Eily's cottage was. He had so much to tell them all, about the fire, and the Bucklands, and his two horses. Another mile or two and he would see the whitewash of his sister's cottage, where old Aunt Nano would make him sit down like a travelling storyteller and go through all that had happened. He grinned to himself, longing to see them all again.

Frank Murphy

from

LOCKIE AND DADGE

'What's your name?' the man asked, and he continued at once, 'Oh, I forgot. You don't remember.'

Lockie remained silent.

'Don't worry, boy, you'll remember in time, but you must have a name. I can't call you if you don't have a name. Would you mind if I gave you a name?'

'What name?' Lockie asked doubtfully.

'Moses,' said the man, grinning as if he had solved the riddle of the universe. 'I think that's a good name. Suitable too.'

'I don't like it,' said Lockie. He had always wanted to know who he really was. Having yet another name would make him feel even more of a nobody, as if any old name would do him.

'But it's the right name for you,' the man said. 'Do you know what "Moses" means? "Taken from the water." That's what it means. And isn't that what you were? Taken from the water.'

Lockie didn't answer. The man went to the cart and took out a camping stove. He lit the jets. He filled a billy can and a tin can with water from a large plastic container and set them to boil on the stove.

'But I've no name for you,' Lockie said. 'What will I call you?'

'Call me Dadge to rhyme with badge or cadge,' the man answered.

'That's a funny name.'

'Short for *Adagio*. Something to do with slow music. A young lad called me that one day. We had done near forty miles that day, and when we got to the village of Knocknamona in the County Kerry, poor old Rosie was ready to drop. The village street is on a steep hill, and the unfortunate animal was hardly able to put one foot in front of another, never mind pull the cart up the hill. If you saw us, you'd be hard put to know whether we were going forward or backwards or stopped entirely.'

Dadge went to the cart and took out a large canvas bag. From it he drew enamelled mugs and plates, spoons, a knife, and laid them on the ground before them.

Then he continued, 'I had to get down off the cart and walk at Rosie's head. A young lad came out of a house, a young lad carrying a fiddle case. He stood on the footpath and stared at us, and then he began to laugh – out loud. People came out and stood at their doors to watch us going by. The young lad pointed at me and shouted, "Look at him, *Adagio*!" The name stuck and later on it got shortened to "Dadge".'

Soon they were eating. Lockie was so hungry that it was as good as a feast. The slightly salted butter and brown bread were delicious. The tea was strong and sweet. He loved the smoky flavour of the tea and the picnic feel of the meal.

When they had finished, Dadge went over to the funny-looking donkey and stroked her neck. She tossed her head and continued browsing the grass. Dadge checked the rope which tethered her to the bush. He put some fresh wood on the fire and came and sat down.

'What kind of a horse is Rosie?' Lockie asked.

'Everyone knows that isn't a horse. It's a jennet.'

'What's a jennet?'

'A jennet is a kind of donkey.'

'What kind of a donkey?'

'A donkey with a pony for a father, if you know what I mean,' Dadge said.

Lockie said nothing, though he still wasn't quite sure what a jennet was.

'What are you doing out here with a jennet and cart?' he asked.

'That cart is my mobile home,' Dadge said, and he raised his eyebrows and threw a glance at

Lockie. 'The jennet is my tractor for pulling the mobile home from one place to another.'

'That's crazy. You'd be killed by the big lorries flying along the road every day, and speed hogs in sports cars.'

'I don't go near the big roads,' said Dadge as he poked aimlessly with a stick at the red embers. 'When I have to go on a main road, I leave it all to Rosie. She's a wise old jennet. She knows how to stay in by the grass margin, and she takes no notice of the noise.'

'It's still a mad way to travel,' Lockie insisted. 'Why don't you get a van?'

'A van!' Dadge said, and Lockie could hear the contempt in his voice. 'Even if I could afford one, I wouldn't want it.'

'Why not?'

Dadge stopped poking the fire and looked at Lockie. 'Think for a minute, Moses,' he said. 'Suppose I had a van, would I get to see the countryside when I was flying by?'

'You might if you went slow enough.' Lockie was trying to divert Dadge from thinking about what should be done with himself.

'Slow or fast,' Dadge said, 'I'd have to watch the road in case a bigger fool than myself was coming against me.'

Lockie had run out of things to say, but he wanted to keep the debate going. He turned over and rested on his left elbow.

'I still think it's crazy,' he said.

'Why so?'

'It's too slow.'

'What's the hurry?' Dadge said dreamily as he gazed at the fire. 'Don't you know it's nicer to be going somewhere than getting there.'

Again Lockie was at a loss. He had no answer to that.

'Nobody goes around on a cart nowadays,' he said in one final, feeble effort to distract Dadge.

'You're wrong there, Moses. I do.'

'But no one else.'

A silence followed, and Lockie's main concern kept nagging at him. He decided to get it over with.

'What are you going to do?' he asked.

'How do you mean?'

'What are you going to do about me?'

Dadge thought for a while. 'I don't know yet. First I want to find out who you are. Then I can be thinking what I should do about you. But now it's getting late and we must sleep.'

Dadge stood up and looked at the sky.

'It's going to be a fine night,' he said, 'a light wind and clear skies. But it'll be cold before morning, and the dew will be heavy. We must be well wrapped up.'

He went to the cart and got a sleeping bag and

several rolls of tarpaulin.

'That's yours,' he said, handing the sleeping bag to Lockie. 'Stretch it out there for yourself and get into it.'

When Lockie was in the bag, Dadge put a bundle of clothing under the flap to make a pillow. Then he took a few sticks from the heap of firewood and hammered them into the ground near the boy's head. A piece of tarpaulin laid over the sticks made a small cave-like shelter.

'How's that now?' he asked.

'Great,' Lockie answered.

He was cosy and warm in his sleeping bag. He was excited about sleeping in the open air for the first time in his life and forgot to worry about what was going to happen to him. His head was raised slightly on the 'pillow' and he could look out of his little cave at the sky. Already it was pierced by a single bright star.

Dadge was busy about the hollow, making his bed with sheets of tarpaulin and old clothes, stowing things away in the cart. Lockie heard him go up the slope and say a few soft words to the jennet. There was a hissing and crackling as Dadge dowsed the fire. Then Lockie could hear him settling into his own 'sleeping bag' a yard or two to his left.

The sky darkened slowly, and, as it did, more stars peeped through. One by one they came at first. Then they came in clusters, so fast that where one moment a patch of dark sky was opaque, an instant later it was peppered with pinpricks of light. Soon the whole heaven had deepened to a dark navy and it was riddled with stars.

'Pins and needles,' Lockie said aloud. Talking to himself at night was a habit he had developed over the years.

'What's that?' Dadge asked.

'I was just thinking. The sky looks like it has pins and needles.'

'It does too, boy. It does. Stop thinking now, and go to sleep.'

Lockie closed his eyes, and his ears and mind began to adapt to a new set of night sounds. There was almost a total quiet apart from the hush and muffled drumming of the sea as the waves collapsed gently on the shore.

'Dadge,' he called.

'What is it?'

'About tomorrow ...'

'Tomorrow is tomorrow. We can do nothing about tomorrow until it comes. Now go to sleep.'

Later a piercing cry brought Lockie half-awake.

'What's that?'

'A curlew.'

He half-opened his eyes and saw the sky still filled with stars. He felt reassured and dropped back into a deep, sound sleep.

C*★★*.

Maeve Friel

from

DISTANT VOICES

A fleet of the foreigners came into Lough Foyle
... Cennrig was quickly abandoned by them,
except for a few who remained behind in it through
sloth ... Fergal, son of Domnall, King of the North,
was in hostilities with them, and killed the crew of
one of their ships and took its booty.

The Annals of Ulster, 920 AD

Only you will know where to find me.
Ellie opened her eyes. A tall boy-man was
standing at her bedroom window, his slim face and
golden hair caught in a pool of ghostly green
moonlight.
My name is Harald Olafsson, he said, turning to
face her with his startling blue eyes. *You must give
me leave to speak to you. You have no need to fear
me.*
Ellie raised her head from her pillow and rubbed
her eyes. Was someone there or was she still

dreaming? The boy looked at her, his expression so sad and wretched that she felt she must reach out and comfort him, but the figure floated out into the starry night without another word.

Night-time had always been vividly alive for Ellie – her dreams came thick and fast as soon as she hit the pillow and continued through the night until the first proop-proop of the alarm clock woke her. Some nights the familiar faces of her family and friends were crowded out by less well-known ones, people on the margins of her life like shop assistants, dimly remembered faces from her childhood, even, sometimes, the casualties of the random bombings and murders that fleeted across the television screen nightly – she imagined her brain frantically sifting through her life each night, recording everything, filing it all away for posterity.

Recently though, something strange and puzzling was happening – her dreams were so different they felt alien, out of character. It was almost as if they didn't belong to her. This voice, this Harald, was haunting her dreams, speaking to her in his strange accent, drawing her into another life, forcing her to listen ... She began to feel as if he had burrowed beneath her skin and was using her sleep to spin dreams thronged with strange men from long ago, their distant voices straining to be heard.

Each night now, for over a week, she had been dreaming of a ship, following its journey across the ocean. It came, she knew, from a wild and barren place, sailing swiftly across the sea where whales loomed and large seabirds circled and screamed above the sails. Harald stood next to the captain at the rudder. He was tall and broad-shouldered but his long slim face was still clean-shaven, with just a sprinkling of fine hairs on his upper lip. He had blond hair, so pale it was almost white, which he wore held back at the nape of his neck in a long ponytail. On the seventh night, he smiled and stretched out an arm to take her hand, but she shrank away from his touch and opened her eyes. The figure stood by the window, beckoning to her, as real and life-like as the figure in her dream, but as she raised her head from the pillow, he floated out into the night.

Ellie fell back into a fitful sleep, drifting in and out of dreams. Several times the scene shifted to a wide sandy beach, a place she half recognised but could not name. It was pitch-black to begin with but as her eyes became used to the darkness, she made out a crowd of people moving across the sand dunes. There was a high wind howling, stirring up the sea into white horses, making her shiver even in sleep. The tide was coming in fast, throwing itself against the cliff in thunderous bursts of spray.

Ellie was floating, looking down on the strand as if she were drifting above it in a hot-air balloon, conscious that at any moment she might come crashing down to earth. Suddenly great tongues of orange fire lit up the whole beach and the sand dunes behind. A vast bonfire had been set ablaze on the shore. In the flames Ellie could make out the dark shape of a ship around which the strange figures danced and ran, many of them wailing and crying out in a language she could not understand. A number of men approached the ship, carrying wooden shields which they beat with long sticks to drown the wailing of the dancing women. Others began to move forward, each bearing a burning piece of wood which they threw on the pyre. The wind grew stronger and more terrifying, fanning the fire on the ship so that the blazing timbers creaked and groaned. Deep in sleep, Ellie's hand brushed her cheek to wipe away the splinters of sooty wood which the wind carried across the beach. The air was thick with the smell of burning resin and the salt of the sea.

She struggled to wake, and lay tossing and turning in her bed, listening to the wind howling outside and rattling the windowpanes. She heard the Guildhall clock strike five o'clock, then the quarter hour and the half hour. Some time later she must have drifted back to sleep only to take up the dream where it had ended.

The burning ship had turned to ash. She began to walk towards it, feeling underfoot the spiky blades of marram grass pricking her bare feet. As she drew closer, the heat coming off the charred timbers burned her cheeks and scorched the back of her throat so that she stopped and raised a hand to shield her face. She was astonished to find her cheeks wet with tears.

You're not dreaming any more, whispered the voice of Harald. *Come and find me*, he said. *Only you will know where to look.*

Once more Ellie forced herself to waken up: she *would* not listen any longer to the voice. At first she lay buried beneath the duvet, too scared to look into the room for fear of what she might see – but the voice would not go away. It called her name, repeating it again and again in a soothing hypnotic tone until finally she could ignore it no longer. She slipped out of bed and moved, trance-like, to the window.

Not a being stirred in the city. She looked down on the river, full and grey in the early morning light. It was moving swiftly, engorged by the recent heavy rains so that it almost lapped the lower deck of the bridge, and swelling in a wide s-shaped curve as it passed out of the city towards the lough beyond. As she watched, her blood froze.

A spectral fleet of six sailing ships was advancing up the river. Each bore one huge square sail behind which the wind screamed. They glided over the surface of the water like a group of monstrous invincible swans but as they came closer, Ellie could see that the long necks of their prows ended not in the graceful head of a bird, but in the snarling, bare-toothed sneer of dogs and dragons.

Am I still dreaming, she thought. Is this a dream within a dream? She shut her eyes tightly and wished herself back into consciousness. No, she was not dreaming any more. Gingerly she drew the side of her hand across the cold wet condensation on the windowpane and peered through the smear. The ships were still there and coming closer. She blinked again to make the image fade and rubbed her eyes. The city on the other side of the river seemed to shimmer in the light and fade away. The quays, the bridge, the cathedral spires disappeared. Now the soft rounded hills behind grew darker and more wooded. The familiar landscape that Ellie had grown up with, the contours and shadows of the city she had looked across at every day since she had been old enough to be aware of the world outside her window, seemed to shrink. Finally all that was left was a cluster of low buildings perched on one hill with the river circling around them. The modern city had vanished, leaving nothing but the island in the middle of the river.

I am dreaming, thought Ellie, even though I think I am not. She turned back: her room was exactly as she expected – the duvet lying at the base of the bed where she had flung it, the walls lined with the faces of musicians and actors, the green hands of the alarm clock showing ten to six. She put her face close up against the window and stared out into the darkness. Down on the river below the ships sailed relentlessly towards the city on its tiny island.

As Ellie looked on transfixed, two cormorants, flying in low over the water, landed on a rock mid-stream and stretched their stiff black wings, spreading them out to dry, like two witches of the sea holding their cloaks aloft. On the opposite bank, a large silver-backed wolf slunk out from the shadow of the trees and bared its teeth at the advancing ships beneath.

Suddenly there was a mighty shout that echoed over the river and startled the black birds which flew off low over the water. The sailors, so close now that she could see their bearded faces, seized their oars, hitting the water in short rapid strokes that stirred the river up into a milky foam. They were steering straight for shore, heading directly for the bank beneath her.

Ellie cried out and turned back into the room. At that moment the Guildhall clock began to ring, its chimes welcome and familiar. From far off she

heard the hum of the army helicopter as it set off on its early morning patrol over the city. The wind had started up again, pelting the windowpane with large raindrops. She looked down towards the river-bank again. There were no strange ships. The Foyle snaked blackly past the sleeping city with its familiar landmarks, both old and new. There was the slender spire of the cathedral, there the green dome of the department store in The Diamond, and there the massive swaying arms of a crane rising above a building site on the quays.

What is happening to me? Was I sleep-walking? Did I dream those ships? Baffled and a bit frightened, Ellie sat down on the edge of her bed, trying to steady her breath which came in short painful gasps. A voice – a voice which might have been Harald's – was echoing in her ears. *Beware the curse of Fenri*, it said. She repeated the phrase aloud, trying to make sense of it. Who or what was Fenri? What did it mean? Had she just imagined the ghostly figure at the window, the phantom fleet of Viking warriors? Or had she truly seen a ghost?

She lay back against the pillow. Her head ached and her limbs felt exhausted as if she had been running all night long but she fought the waves of tiredness that flowed over her. She would not allow herself to sleep again. With eyes stretched wide, she stared at the ceiling above her bed, fighting

back the images of the strange world of the foreign
sailors. You are in your own room, safe and secure,
she told herself. Nothing bad can happen here. She
repeated the phrases to herself, as if the saying of
them might be enough to make them true. A loose
corner of peeling wallpaper flapped in the draught
from the window. The water tank suddenly
juddered and gurgled. A car sped past the house,
its headlamps briefly illuminating the room. This is
normal, she thought, this is the real world – it was
just a dream I had, nothing but a dream. Above her
head, the cracks in the plaster of the old ceiling
seemed to roll and shift, flowing like vast
continental rivers towards the central light bulb,
throwing out tributaries which snaked down the
sides of the dormer window. Immediately the
picture of Harald and his ghost-ships gliding up the
Foyle reappeared and she shuddered. She felt
possessed, as if someone had crept beneath her
skin, manufacturing her dreams, compelling her
to watch them.

C☽*★*★*.

Tom McCaughren

from

IN SEARCH OF THE LIBERTY TREE

Rooks were swirling above the woods of the Adair demesne like dark clouds gathering in a sunny sky. Beneath them, Sammy and Joshua ran through the trees for all they were worth, just as they had done on another sunny day a long time ago, before all the trouble had begun. This time they weren't racing each other, but trying to get ahead of a column of Government troops which had marched up through the town.

When they reached the field inside the entrance they were in time to see several hundred bayonets flashing in the sun, as the troops, who had lined up in long rows, shouldered their muskets.

'Quick,' whispered Joshua, 'give me a leg up.'

Sammy helped Joshua climb into the nearest tree and was in turn pulled up after him. From their vantage point, they now had a panoramic view of the assembled troops. Some, they could see, were regular soldiers from England, others

members of the Monaghan Militia. All wore bright
red tunics, and as he looked down on them Joshua
couldn't help thinking that the tunics were like
stains of blood on the green of the grass. Perhaps it
was because he was thinking of Constable
Crawford and how he would have come out of the
porter's lodge to let the troops in. Maybe it was
because he had been thinking of Master Davison
and how he himself would have been at school now
that it was Monday morning, if the master had
been alive. Or perhaps it was the thought of the
dead yeoman he had fallen over behind the Market
House. He wasn't sure but, whatever it was, the red
tunics reminded him of the colour of blood.

In front of the troops, several officers sat astride
their horses, some of which bowed and pranced as
the last of the troops moved into position. From
the handles of their sabres hung gold and silver
tassels which rolled with the movement of the
horses and, like the bayonets, glinted whenever
they caught a ray of sun. Only a few days before, the
same tassels had been wrapped around their wrists
to ensure that the swords would stay in their hands
as they slashed at the rebels in Antrim town. But
for now the swords were in their scabbards, the
tassels an impressive decoration.

Sammy and Joshua had left Gracehill with their
parents when word had arrived that those
inhabitants of Ballymena who didn't return would

be regarded as rebels and their houses burned. The rebels, they found, had lost all heart for the fight when news of the defeat at Antrim had reached them, and when Government troops had appeared on the hills they had melted back into the countryside, leaving the townspeople to face the wrath of the army.

'There's my father,' said Joshua.

A group of people had now entered the demesne and were walking over to the officers who were still on horseback. Besides Mr Watson, they could see that the deputation included other people of some standing in the town.

'I wonder what they're saying?' said Sammy.

'I don't know,' Joshua replied. 'But whatever it is, my father doesn't look very pleased about it.'

A few moments later the deputation turned and walked away. The officers waited until they had gone out through the gates, then brought their horses round to face their men. With shouted orders, the soldiers were dismissed, and Sammy whispered, 'Come on. We'd better get out of here. If they spot us, they might think we're spying on them. And you heard what happened to the weaver's son in Randalstown.'

Joshua nodded. They had heard that several people, including a boy their own age, had been shot and killed during house searches in Randalstown. There was no way of knowing if it was true, but now, as some of the soldiers began to wander close to the tree where they were hiding, they scrambled down as fast as they could, and made a beeline for the boundary wall.

When they returned to the inn, they found Mr Watson helping Moses to load provisions on to the cart in the stable yard.

'What's happening?' panted Joshua.

Mr Watson wiped the sweat from his brow with his forearm. His other arm was still in a sling. 'Colonel Clavering has demanded that we provide his troops with food and drink.'

'Here, we'll do that,' said Sammy, and the two of them helped Moses to lift a bag of flour up on to the cart.

'But sure there's hardly anything left,' said Joshua. 'The rebels have taken most of it.'

'We've no choice,' his father explained. 'Either we give them what we have, or they come and take it.'

'But what about the amnesty?' asked Joshua.

'It's the United Irishmen who are getting the amnesty,' said Mr Watson. 'All we're getting is the blame.'

'Do you mean they're all getting off scot-free?' asked Sammy.

'Not all of them,' said Moses.

'The amnesty doesn't apply to the leaders,' said Mr Watson. 'Or, I would imagine, to anyone else they can prove was involved. They're setting up their headquarters in Castle Street. All offenders will be tried by military court.'

'What does that mean?' asked Joshua.

'It means,' his father told him, 'that they're going to hang them.'

'But how will they know who was involved?' asked Sammy.

'The United Irishmen weren't the only ones in town,' said Moses. He pushed the bag of flour into place on the cart, and added, 'You can rest assured the Government had their spies here too.'

'They're probably drawing up a list of troublemakers at this very moment,' said Mr Watson. 'And all I can say is, God help them.'

Within hours, Colonel Clavering had set up his headquarters in the premises in Castle Street used by the yeomen and, as if to add insult to injury, his troops installed themselves in the town's two places of worship – the parish church in Church Street, and the Presbyterian meeting-house. Then, acting on the information of their spies, the troops moved into action.

Sammy's father had returned to his loom and, after a long day's work, had gone to bed with his family in the loft opposite the fire. He was happy to be back at work, and was thinking that weaving was much more to his liking than rebellion when there was loud hammering on the cabin door.

'All right, all right,' he shouted. 'I'm coming.'

His wife sat up and watched him climb down the ladder to open the door. 'Be careful, Nathaniel,' she whispered. 'You wouldn't know who's abroad these nights.'

Sammy, too, was sitting up. The rebel leaders were still at large and he feared it might be Archer and Dr Linn, calling again to punish his father for not taking an active part in the rebellion.

No sooner had Mr Johnston unbolted the top half of the door than it was flung back, and several bayonets were thrust at his throat. A militiaman reached in to unbolt the lower half, and before he knew what was happening they had pushed in on top of him.

Seeing her husband lying on the floor, a hand raised to try and protect himself from the sharp points of the bayonets, Mrs Johnston screamed. A militiaman immediately climbed the ladder and threw back the clothes to see who else might be there. Now awake, the children also screamed, and Sammy shouted, 'There's no one else here, only the children.'

'You,' said the militiaman, pointing his bayonet at Sammy. 'You come down here too.'

Mrs Johnston pleaded, but her cries, like those of her children, were in vain. Sammy and his father were allowed to delay only long enough to pull on their breeches before they were marched out into the night.

By morning it became clear that Mr Johnston had been on a very long list of names supplied to the military by Government spies. Many other cabins had been raided during the night and the menfolk arrested. Some cabins in outlying areas had also been burned. As a result, Mrs Johnston was only one of a number of women who came to the inn, seeking the help of Mr Watson in locating their husbands and sons.

Elizabeth O'Hara

from

THE HIRING FAIR

The third of November was a bleak, blustery day. All over the square of the small town of Milford, children and their parents huddled together for shelter from the north-east wind that whistled through the lanes and alleys. It whipped at Sally's ears and chin and nose, turning them purple with cold.

She and Katie stood with their mother on the pavement outside Diamond's public house. They had said goodbye to Janey at home, trying to hide from her the fact that they would not see her again for six months. That this year, they would not be at home to see what Father Christmas brought her, or to bring her sliding on the frozen lake in the middle of the mountains during the cold spell that always came in January. They pretended they were going to Milford to shop at the fair. This was not exactly tactful, because Janey wanted to go too. Shopping was her favourite activity. The word 'fair' filled her mind with the taste of sweets, to which she was helplessly addicted, and with visions of toys, which she hardly ever got, but which she loved. It was enough to make anyone scream, the thought of missing all that. And she did scream, and howl, and dance up and down on the floor. In the end the neighbour who had come to look after her had to pin her down on her lap and ask her own son to guard the door while Sally and Katie and their mother made their escape. The last sound in their ears as they left home was the sound of their little sister's screams of frustration, mixed up with Granny's grunts from the bed and the cackling of the hens.

And now, the hiring fair. It was not amusing, at least not in the sense that Janey anticipated. What was for sale were not sweets and toys, but men, women and children. Half the people who were crowding the big grey square were waiting to be 'hired': that is, they wanted to be employed by farmers from Tyrone and Derry, or from farther afield, for the next six months. They would sell their services for a few pounds, say goodbye to their homes and friends, and set off to live and work among strangers. In many instances, they would not know what to expect in their new places of employment. They might be well or badly treated. The next six months might be heaven or hell. Only one thing was certain: they were going to be far away from everything and everyone they knew best. For the six months, to all intents and purposes they would be owned by the farmers who would hire them today.

Many of the people waiting to be hired were children, some of them much younger than Sally and Katie. A boy standing next to them with his father and mother looked about seven years old, and some of the other children were not much older. Sally, at thirteen, and Katie at eleven, were amongst the biggest children in the square: 'children', because Mrs Gallagher had dressed them in their pinafores and black stockings, to emphasise their youth. Their new grown-up frocks were packed in the little baskets that lay at their feet. 'Only for Sundays!' their mother had admonished, wagging her finger. But the real reason she asked them to wear their pinafores was that she wanted them to be treated as children and not as adults by their new bosses. Even though they would earn more money as grown-ups, they would have to work harder for it. She thought it was all hard enough as it was.

It was only nine o'clock. The Gallaghers had set off from home before six. One of their neighbours, Paddy Friel, had given them a ride in his donkey and cart half-way to the town and they had walked the rest of the way, a distance of about four miles. It had been a slow, painful journey, with the wind and rain slapping against their faces and their bags weighing down their backs.

Sally patted her basket, trying to get some comfort from it. Inside there was a change of underwear, two nightdresses and her Sunday frock and shoes. Besides, she had packed a jotter and pencil, and her copy of *Uncle Tom's Cabin*. She had already read the latter, but had enjoyed it so much and spoken of it in such glowing terms that Miss Lynch had presented it to her before she left home. She did not say what she was thinking: that there might not be many books in the place Sally was going to. But Sally guessed her thoughts: the same idea had already occurred to her, although she was hoping for the best. After all, you never knew your luck! Miss Lynch had hugged Sally then, and told her to be brave.

It had only been yesterday. Already it seemed a lifetime away. Thousands of miles from this awful place, where farmers were already marching purposefully around, looking prospective servants up and down, pinching their muscles and feeling their bones to test their strength. It was too like the slave markets described in the book Sally had in her bag – and in her head – to be palatable.

A large man wearing knee breeches and a black three-cornered hat came up to Mrs Gallagher and asked her if the girls were hers.

'Are they your weans?' was what he said,

actually. Sally understood what he said, but with difficulty: she was not used to hearing English spoken except by children and the teacher, in school. Irish was the language all ordinary grown-ups spoke at home.

Mrs Gallagher nodded, unable to speak in the first shock of experiencing what she had been dreading for weeks.

'Stand out here, you!' he pointed at Katie with his stick.

Katie, ever obedient, stepped meekly forward.

He looked her up and down, then walked around and examined her from the back. His face was red and there was a big mole on his chin with tufts of red wiry hair growing out of it. On his breath was the unmistakable smell of whiskey: most of the farmers in Milford smelt of it, since the public houses opened early especially for the fair.

'Not a bad wee lassie!' he said, his examination over. Sally breathed a sigh of relief on Katie's behalf. At least she was not going to be pinched or measured, as some of the children were.

Mrs Gallagher had by now picked up enough courage to look him in the eye.

'Aye, Mam, she's a fine wean. How much are you looking for her?'

'Eight pounds,' said Mrs Gallagher in a surprisingly firm tone.

The man scratched his head, lifting his cap

slightly in order to get at the itchiest bits.

'There's them that cost less,' he said after a few moments' happy scratching.

Mrs Gallagher said absolutely nothing. Sally and Katie watched, spellbound by this interplay. They had hardly ever heard their mother speaking English, or display such confidence. Where had she got it from? If she was putting on an act, it was certainly a convincing one. So engrossed were they in her performance, if that's what it was, that for a moment they forgot that it was Katie who was the object of the bargaining.

'Of course, she's a fine lassie, and a good worker, I'll be bound.'

Mrs Gallagher spoke: 'She's one of the best workers going. She can milk and churn. She can spin and sew and dye and knit. She can bake bread and wash clothes and look after children better than most women twice her age.'

'Hm!' the man scratched his head again, but in a business-like, not a thoughtful, way this time. 'I believe you!' he said with a grin. 'I'll take her, even at eight pounds! Them that buys cheap buys dear, my mother always says, and it's my mother who's paying for her.'

Mrs Gallagher stood her ground. Oddly enough, in spite of the horror with which they had viewed the proceedings, all the Gallaghers were pleased that the man had reached this decision and was happy to pay more than the going rate for Katie. It confirmed their belief that they were better than the run of the mill. Besides, it meant that Mrs Gallagher would already have enough money to pay the rent next time it was due, although she'd be in arrears until then.

'There's a condition!' said Mrs Gallagher.

'What's that?' he asked, taken aback. One did not expect conditions from the likes of these people, especially not when they'd already driven a hard bargain.

'This is the first time these girls have been away from home. I want both of them to be hired in the same neighbourhood.'

'Begob, madam, that is easier said than done!' said the man, with a disbelieving laugh. 'I need one maid, not half a dozen!'

'If you can't arrange for the other girl to go with her sister, you can't have either of them,' said Mrs Gallagher.

'It's all right, Mother,' Katie began to say.

Mrs Gallagher stopped her.

'No, Katie, it's not all right. We'll do it this way. It will work, you mark my words. I'll not have you going off all alone. That's the least I can do for you!'

The farmer was still looking at Katie, and from her to Sally. Finally he said, 'I'll see what I can do. There's a neighbour of mine about the place somewhere, William Stewart by name. There's a chance he might take the other wee lass, although I know for a fact it's a grown woman he's looking for.'

'Ask him if he's interested,' said Mrs Gallagher. 'We'll stay here. If you're not back in half an hour we'll take it that you're not interested.'

The man smiled to himself and went off. They watched him cross the square and look around. Soon he disappeared into a pub.

'That's the last we'll see of him, probably!' said Mrs Gallagher. 'But don't you worry, there'll be others.'

They had to wait for half an hour before going on the market again. During that time, several men came up and looked at the girls with interest. Mrs Gallagher told them all to come back after ten o'clock.

'The best ones are always gone!' said one of the farmers, an exceptionally tall man, with a confident air and a handsome face. Sally wished she could go to work for him, but when she mentioned this to her mother she said, 'He's the last one I'd hire you to. He looks like a conceited pup.'

Sally stared at the young farmer as he strode majestically through the throng. His eyes glistened, and so did his boots. He was the most smartly dressed farmer at the fair. But he did, as

Mrs Gallagher said, look a bit stuck up. His expression, as he examined the people up for hire, was haughty.

The little boy next to them, whose name, they had learned by listening, was Johnny, was looked over by many farmers and rejected by all of them as being too small. Johnny and his parents became increasingly dismayed, and Sally, although she secretly hoped that Johnny would not be employed, since he looked much too young to have to leave his parents, felt sorry for them. In the end a big rough farmer wearing thick tweeds came and examined Johnny minutely. He asked Johnny what age he was and Johnny said, 'Ten.'

'Small for your age,' the farmer said suspiciously.

'You can have him for four pounds, sir,' said Johnny's father, a small thin man with a scabby face. 'He's a grand wee worker, a great lad.'

'He's small,' said the farmer. 'Here, young fellow, can you lift that?'

And he threw a large sack of potatoes at Johnny's feet.

Making an enormous effort, Johnny hoisted it onto his shoulders. Sally and Katie could see that he almost burst with the attempt and began to hate his parents, especially his father, who had a weak, whining voice. Sally hoped against hope that the farmer would not take him.

But he did. Johnny, however small, was cheap at four pounds. A bargain offer. The last they saw of him was him running along beside the horse of the farmer, carrying a heavy bag and crying his eyes out. Tears came to their own eyes, looking at him. His own parents did not see: they had left the marketplace as soon as the bargain was made, and had gone into one of the public houses.

The Gallaghers sat glumly on their baskets for some time after this, trying to forget the picture of poor little Johnny running for all he was worth alongside the fat farmer on his horse.

'Maybe he has a kind wife,' said Sally, finally, with an attempt at optimism.

'He doesn't look like a man who has a kind wife!' said Katie.

'You wouldn't know,' said Mrs Gallagher. 'Kind women often marry the most awful men. It is a thing I've noticed.'

At that moment, the man who had spoken with them earlier returned, bringing with him his friend – none other than the farmer Sally had admired.

'This is William Stewart,' said the farmer. 'And my own name, by the way, is Robert Campbell. Willie here has agreed to take on the big girl, and I'll take the wee one.'

'Her name is Katie. Katie Gallagher. And the big girl is Sally.'

'Aye. Katie. I'll take Katie here. It's a

companion for me ould mother I'm looking for to tell ye the truth. She's getting on and she needs a nice wee girl to help her around the house and so on, ye know what I mean?'

Now that he had decided on hiring Katie, Mr Campbell was much more talkative than hitherto. He seemed to be regarding the Gallaghers almost as equals.

'And what does Mr Stewart want?' asked Mrs Gallagher, suspiciously.

'Och, just a girl about the house and byre, you know. My wife could do with someone to give her a hand in the dairy. And with the weans.'

'How many children have you?' asked Mrs Gallagher, in a less suspicious tone.

'We've three now, madam, and a fourth on the way. We'll be needing a hand then too.'

Robert Campbell went on to explain that he and William Stewart lived less than half a mile from one another, in a village called Ballygowl, in Tyrone.

'No need to worry about your girls, ma'am,' he went on. 'They'll be well looked after with us, never you fear. And they'll be sent back here on the thirtieth of April, safe and sound. Never you worry about them.'

'All right,' said Mrs Gallagher finally. 'They can go.'

'Don't worry about them, ma'am,' said Mr Campbell, a kind note coming into his husky voice.

'They'll be all right. We'll treat them well enough.'

'They're good girls,' said Mrs Gallagher. But her voice let her down. She couldn't say anything more. Tears streamed down her cheeks as she hugged Sally and Katie and watched them set off with their new employers. She felt even sadder than she had when Jack had drowned.

Sam McBratney

from

THE CHIEFTAIN'S DAUGHTER

I, Dinn Keene, stayed on Grey Man Mountain for not less than five years and not more than seven. I quickly forgot my mother's face and the comfort of my father's sturdy dwelling on the far plains. Instead I had the new-found companionship of Chief Ruadh's hut.

There were no such things as rooms in Ruadh's hut, no private places, no partitions. The fire belched smoke in the middle of the floor. Seven people slept there with two hairy hounds that growled if you took their place, and on the coldest nights goats were admitted also.

Ruadh himself was a powerful, stubby man, so proud of his badger coat that he rarely left it off his back. When he drank crab-apple wine he got down on all fours and bit the dogs. It was Ruadh who taught me how to cast a sling, stalk deer, land fish and braid hair. His own hair, like Corag Mor's, was the colour of the leaves that winter on the trees. I loved him. He used to say that when my real father came to take me back, he was going to give him someone else – one of the bad, good-for-nothing children of the camp. This was a great game. The children used to run away from him, screaming, 'No, not me, not me!'

Everyone there was important to me. I could easily say much about old Breasal, who said songs; Eithne who was in charge of marrow bones; the fearsome Bodman Tar; young Ennis the archer; my friend Oscar. But I must speak now of my lovely Frann.

She was Ard Bruill's daughter. Somehow her memory has stayed fresh with me. I can fairly give her a spray of fine hair the colour of hay, but with more lustre. Often she wove a sprig of heather into her braids, and thus decorated, would come away with Oscar and me to hang upside down from the branches of trees. I did not like Oscar to look at her too closely. I used to poke him with the butt end of my spear for looking too closely.

I remember that Frann had a roving curiosity about all things. On our way to fish or fetch water she would suddenly stop, and call us over to examine something like a trail of slug-slime or a curtain of ice in the depths of a hedge. She was a lithe and eager creature when we played chasing games, and how it made her miserable to lose! She had scars on both knees and was skilled with the sling.

Such was Frann. I came to understand that she had eyes in the back of her head, for she would whip round suddenly, and say, 'Who do *you* think you're looking at, Dinn Keene?'

I had been in the mountains two or three years when I realised that I must do something about this girl who was always in my thoughts. In some way I had to establish that I was her special friend – certainly more special than Oscar, whom I thought of as a great rival. But what could I do? I had neither the words for my vague feelings nor the courage to make them completely public. Some action was called for to make me significant – certainly more significant than Oscar!

One night, lying with my back to one of the goats, I had the idea. I will give her my green sucking blanket, thought Dinn Keene.

This is what happened.

Dinn Keene waited patiently until one morning Breasal came to the door of her hut and called out to Frann, 'Here, take this pot and get me some nettle-heads.'

'Me?' said Frann, who was fondling the ears of her spoiled dog. I was jealous of the beast, and wished I had ears like him.

'Well, I'm not talking to the *dog*,' said Breasal. 'I'll get stung.'

'You'll get stung if you don't, my girl!'

Dinn Keene followed her. The blanket was under his arm, rolled up in a rush mat. He stalked her as if she were a wild beast, and his heart pounded so much that he trembled at the edges of his body.

And then, in the glade which is known as Ulmar's Great Snare, she heard him behind her, and turned.

'What are you doing there, Dinn Keene?'

'I was trying to catch up with you.'

'You were sneaking up on me.'

'I wasn't sneaking up on you, I want to give you something. Here.'

Dinn Keene saw at once that he had surprised her with his generosity. As she took the rush mat and spilled the contents to the ground, her eyelids flickered in wonder. Of course, the blanket was no longer in perfect order, but still, it was far superior to anything that Eithne could produce by her simple weaving.

'Why are you giving me this?' she asked.

Because it is my only possession, thought Dinn Keene. Because I have guarded it tooth and nail against dogs and goats and people since I came to this place.

'I don't really want it any more.'

'But it's your sucking blanket.'

'It's not my sucking blanket.'

'It is so.'

'I don't suck blankets!' cried Dinn Keene in a rage.

'Well, Oscar says you do. You *used* to.'

At that moment Dinn Keene would have split Oscar like a block of wood had he ventured into the clearing. It was true that he used to fall asleep in Ruadh's tent with a corner of the blanket in his mouth – but only in the beginning, for a little while, until the strangeness wore off him.

'Right!' he said hotly. 'Don't have it, then. I'll take it back and give it to somebody else. Eithne's baby can have it.'

'No,' said Frann, pouncing on the blanket, 'I'll have it. Thank you, Dinn Keene. I have to go now, Breasal wants nettles for soup.'

Dinn Keene wandered home that day as if he had sprouted feathers. Somewhere in the glen his Frann was picking nettle heads with his blanket round her shoulders like a shawl. He had showed himself to be a very generous person – certainly more generous than Oscar – and the whole affair made him feel good and worthy of being loved.

Until the following day. Dinn Keene returned to the village with water and soon sensed that something was different. Bodman Tar winked at him, and grinned. He was not the only one. Other people smiled in the same mysterious way, and sly Oscar pretended to whistle while watching like a hawk out of one eye.

Now there was in the village a murderous, slobbering beast called Halfwolf. Murta, who looked after it, kept it tethered to a post during the day, away from people, so that the creature would not be spoiled like the other dogs by too much fondling, and only let it go to roam the glens by night. Dinn Keene could not fail to notice that Halfwolf had acquired a new bed. The beast was curled up nose to tail on the green blanket.

The glee on Oscar's face, and the innocence on Frann's, was too much for Dinn Keene. Seizing the nearest useful object, which happened to be a pole, he tried to shift the creature and rake the blanket clear. The hound came out of its doze with a venomous snarl, gripped the pole with its teeth, and shook poor Dinn Keene at the other end from head to foot.

When Dinn Keene saw that he could not even get the pole back, he said to himself: Dinn Keene, you have lost your blanket.

He had lost much more. Bodman Tar sat some way off with a knowing smile on his face, and Murta bowed his head to snigger in his chest. These, and many more, had a good laugh at his red face.

Oscar knew that he wasn't safe when he saw Dinn Keene coming, and took off like a hare. But Frann did not flinch.

'You gave my blanket to that dog.'

'Oscar dared me to.'

'And you did it!'

'Yes, it was mine, you gave it to me because you didn't want it and anyway you can always suck your thumb if you're stuck for something to suck.'

There was only one answer for such a mouthful. His fist smacked into her face, smashing her to the ground.

'It was the only thing I had. It was my only thing!' he screeched at her, lying there propped on one elbow, staring up at him with shock in her eyes and blood oozing from her bottom lip.

'I hate you, Dinn Keene,' she said.

Let her hate me, thought Dinn Keene! He took pleasure from the very strength of her feeling, for he was the cause of it. In a way it made him significant – certainly more significant than Oscar, who at this moment was hiding among the blackberry brakes.

But I must speak to you now (said old Dinn Keene) of Corag Mor. He, too, was a person of great importance in my story.

You will understand that the people of Chief Ruadh's clan, though not humble by nature, well knew that there are powers in this world who are greater than men or armies of men. For this reason they were glad that Corag Mor had returned to them. He understood the ways of the Otherworld better than they did.

Corag Mor took to painting his face. To come upon him suddenly in the wolf-light, gaudy as a poison berry from the neck up, put more fear into me than a real spirit would have done. From time to time he laid an offering in the Round of Stones. He had the power to go on a journey – that is, to sit in the same place without moving while his mind left him. We all shuddered to think what he might be looking at.

One evening a blue flame appeared in the fire. Ruadh, who was a little drunk, called for Corag Mor to examine it.

'There it is! See? What's it doing there? Why is the little devil burning blue?'

'It's probably a drop of fat from the hen you ate,' said Breasal.

'Hen's fat doesn't burn blue. Murta, have you ever seen hen's fat burn blue?'

Murta, after a wink at his wife, replied solemnly. 'I have seen many things in my time, but never that. I've never seen hen's fat burn blue. How about you, Ennis?'

'No,' said Ennis. 'I've seen a pig's fat burn purple, but never blue.'

'There's a reason for everything, you know,' Ruadh said after draining his cup. 'Everything has a reason. Well, Corag Mor? Explain the blue flame.'

'It may be a warning.'

'A warning? Of what?'

'I don't know.'

'How do you know it's a warning, then? It might be anything.'

'The flame is unnatural,' said Corag Mor, 'so there must be an unnatural reason for it. What that reason is ... Who knows?'

'It's hungry,' cried Ruadh, suddenly raising his voice. 'Frann, come here, girl, bring me what's left of the pig lard, this poor fire is hungry.'

'Don't you dare throw good food on that fire!' shouted Breasal.

As Ruadh brightened the fire with the pig lard, I watched what Frann was up to. Using a stick smeared with lard, she coaxed Halfwolf out of his bed until he came to the end of his rope. Then she dashed in quickly, seized my blanket, and made off with it towards Ard Bruill's hut. She's sorry now for what she did to me, I thought.

Meanwhile, round the fire, Corag Mor left the circle and went off alone. The cups were filled again, the fire sizzled, and Breasal completed the joke by saying, 'Huh! You'll not be laughing when you've to make your own broth in future – mark my words!'

When I think what happened two nights later, I am tempted to believe that Corag Mor was right. The blue flame may indeed have been a warning in the fire.

Siobhán Parkinson

from

AMELIA

Amelia often went with Mama to Findlater's shop to get the groceries. The shop was large and cool and it had a special fruity, sugary smell that Amelia loved. The manager always came out from his office behind the shop, if he heard that the Pims were there, to pay his respects. He would lean over the counter, to where the biscuit tins were ranged with their glass lids slanted outwards so that the customer could see the tempting biscuits inside, nestling on their greaseproof-paper beds, and, flipping a lid, he would take out a biscuit and hold it up ceremoniously to Amelia. He was a large plump grey-haired man with old-fashioned sideburns and a large pocket watch that Amelia used to play with when she was little. Mama and Amelia both took wicker baskets, to carry home the things they needed immediately. The rest would be delivered later in the day by cart. They didn't need to carry a purse, as they had an account at the shop, which Papa settled every month.

This day, however, Mr O'Connell didn't make an appearance when Amelia and Mama came into the shop. He must be out, thought Amelia, or else he didn't realise they were there. But the new young shopboy was very attentive. He lifted up the flap of the counter and opened the little half-door and came out to the customer's side of the counter to get a chair for Mama to sit on. Then he went back to his own side of the counter and took a pencil from behind his ear, which he licked, so that he could take down Mama's list.

Mama had a long list of requirements, and the counter was soon quite covered with food and household goods for the Pim family and servants: currants and raisins and prunes and dried apricots, sugar and salt and flour, semolina and rice and macaroni and cornflour and breadsoda, rashers of bacon and plump, damp strings of sausages, a score of eggs, washing soda and cakes of soap and a little bag of blue for whitening linen, sugar soap and borax powder for cleaning, half-a-dozen lemons, half-a-dozen oranges and a pound of bananas, cabbages, cauliflowers, onions, carrots and parsnips from the greengrocery department, and two thin white paper bags of biscuits, plain and fancy, which the shopboy weighed out carefully, adding an extra biscuit in the end, for good measure.

'Can I tempt you to a half-pound of Barry's tea, all the way from Cork?' asked the shopboy helpfully, not liking actually to suggest that Mama had forgotten something.

'Oh, I think you'll find it's come from much further afield than Cork,' said Mama waggishly. 'But no, thank you, we are Pims, the wine and tea merchants. We have our own sources of tea.'

'I'm sorry, Ma'am.' The shopboy blushed deeply. His blush clashed with his bright orange hair, so that he looked quite unattractive. Amelia felt sorry for him. She smiled at him, but he didn't notice.

'That's all right. How could you be expected to know?' said Mama kindly.

'No, it's not that, Ma'am,' said the boy. Then he leant over the counter and said something to Mama that Amelia couldn't hear.

'Oh, not at all, not at all,' said Mama brightly. 'I'm sure it's some mistake. I'll send my husband in to talk to Mr O'Connell as soon as he gets home and it'll all be settled up in no time. Now don't you feel bad about it at all. I quite understand.'

And Mama turned to leave the shop, taking Amelia by the elbow.

'But, Mama,' said Amelia, digging her heels in, 'we haven't taken the things we'll be needing immediately.'

'There's nothing that we need immediately,' said Mama firmly.

'But, Mama, the biscuits. You said we could have lemon puffs for tea. You promised, Mama.' Amelia thought she was going to cry, and she knew Edmund certainly would when he found out.

'Nonsense, Amelia,' said Mama, steering her daughter out of the shop. 'Lemon cake, I said. Cook's made a lemon cake. I'm sure she said she had.'

Amelia was suspicious. She swung her empty basket as she walked home. If Mama hadn't intended to bring some of the goods home, why had they brought their baskets, she asked herself. But she didn't say anything, just swung her basket pointedly and walked with fierce little steps.

Amelia was right. There was no lemon cake for tea that day, just bread and butter and jam — not even lemon curd. But Mama didn't offer any explanations for her fib, and Amelia knew better than to challenge her.

In any case, Amelia soon forgot all about the episode in Findlaters and the lemon puffs. She had more important things to think about. She and Mama interviewed Mick Moriarty in the back garden on the subject of the orangery roof.

Mick Moriarty took his cap off, using both hands and then replaced it on his head, even further back from his forehead than normal. This was a sign that he was thinking hard. Amelia held her breath.

'Aye,' he said at last, took the cap off again and

replaced it in its normal position over his brow.

Amelia sighed with relief. That meant he thought he could fix it.

It only took him a day – that and a ladder, a football-sized lump of putty, and a few choice curses which Mama pretended not to hear. In between fixing panes in place he would throw the ball of putty down to Amelia, and she would keep it warm and pliable by pulling and rolling it in her hands, while Mick Moriarty did a bit of knife work. The putty was lovely stuff to manipulate, like elastic dough, and it smelt almost good enough to eat.

They left it for a day to harden, and then Amelia and Mary Ann went at the glass with newspapers soaked in methylated spirit. They cleaned every bit of glass as high as they could reach, and Mick Moriarty got his ladder and cleaned the roof for them.

After they had finished, Amelia and Mary Ann stood in the middle of the orangery, from which all the dusty old furniture had been cleared away, in an ankle-deep wash of medicinal-smelling newspapers and admired their sparkling glass-work. The sun obligingly came out and shone with special brilliance through the glass and onto the two girls, making their hair glint and gleam, as if to approve their work.

With a sigh of satisfaction, Amelia helped Mary

Ann to pile the black and sodden newspapers into buckets and carry them through the house to the kitchen, where they poked them into the range. The fire shot up voraciously to eat the spirituous newsprint, and the girls laughed as they fed it more and more papers. Cook caught them at it and threw her hands up in despair, telling them the chimney would catch fire if they didn't look out, but they just laughed at her and stuffed the last few scrunches of newspaper into the range's black mouth.

Then they scrubbed their filthy hands at the scullery sink, and Mary Ann made tea. She used the earthenware kitchen teapot, not the silver one Amelia was used to, and the tea was hot and sweet and strong. They ate bread and dripping with it, which was the normal kitchen teatime fare. Amelia thought it was heaven to sit at the sturdy deal table and eat thick cuts of bread with Mary Ann and Cook, and not have to listen to Edmund breathing in that irritating way of his, or watch Grandmama at her eternal needlepoint and eat daintily in the drawing-room way.

'Isn't this fun, Mary Ann?' she said, even though her mouth was half-full and she should have waited till it was empty.

To Amelia it was like a picnic, but of course to Mary Ann it was nothing special, except that Amelia was there. Even so, Mary Ann said, 'Yes,

Amelia.' There, she'd done it! She'd called her Amelia, without even flinching.

Amelia noticed. She didn't say anything, but she gave Mary Ann an extra-specially warm smile. And Mary Ann grinned back.

And that was how the orangery came to be a crystal dome once more, full of nothing but clear, sparkling air. By now the emerald silk dress was almost ready, Papa had secured the promise of a gramophone, and plans for the food and decorations were well under way. Amelia had a lurching feeling in her insides every time she thought about the party, but she took a deep breath and reminded Mama that it was time to write the invitations.

So they sat down one evening with Papa's best fountain pen and a pile of smooth square white cards edged with gold and wrote notes to all Amelia's classmates and her cousins Louise and Beatrice. 'And Joshua, Mama,' said Amelia.

'Joshua? Oh, I'm sure your cousin Joshua won't want to come to a girls' party.'

'But, Mama, we'll need some boys. For the dancing.'

'Ah, for the dancing,' said Mama with a knowing nod. 'I see. I knew there must be some point to boys. Goodness knows, they're pretty useless otherwise.'

Amelia was too distracted even to notice that

Mama was making a little joke. She chewed Papa's
fountain pen and looked out of the window.

'And what other young men did you have in
mind, Amelia? I don't suppose poor Josh is
expected to do all the honours.'

'Mary Webb has a brother,' said Amelia without
enthusiasm. 'And Dorothea Jacob has a cousin, a
boy-cousin, I mean. Lucinda's brother is almost
sixteen. Do you think that's too old, Mama?'

'I expect he's almost ready to draw a pension,'
said her mother, 'but we could ask him anyway, and
if he can still walk without a stick, perhaps he
might be prevailed upon to come.'

'I can't think of any more,' wailed Amelia. 'Oh,
Mama, have any of your suffragettes got sons?'

'Are you sure that is the sort of boy you want to
mix with, Amelia?' asked her mother wickedly.

'Why, Mama! You're a suffragette.'

'And I'm all right?'

'Oh yes, Mama. Of course you are.'

'I'm pleased to hear it,' said Mama. 'Sometimes,
Amelia, I think you are so disapproving of
everything I do, that I almost feel guilty.'

'Oh, Mother!' said Amelia. 'It's not up to me to
approve or disapprove of what you do.' But she
knew, deep down inside, what her mother meant.

'No, of course it isn't. But still, one doesn't like
to feel one's own daughter thinks one is crackers.'

'Mama, I don't think you're crackers. I think

perhaps you're a little ... well, perhaps a little quick to get involved in things. But not crackers.'

'Ah well,' said Mama. But she didn't finish the sentence.

Just then Papa came into the room, smoking his curly pipe and scenting the air with it. He was in his carpet slippers and had on his comfortable at-home look.

'What are the ladies up to?' he asked in his gallant way.

'Writing invitations, Papa,' said Amelia. 'For the birthday party.'

'Ah, next week!' said Papa, ruffling Amelia's hair.

'Oh, and Papa, can the guests have a ride in the motor-car? I promised.'

'What?' said Papa, in mock horror. 'Do you think I'm running a motorised hackney-cab? Or a funfair ride?'

'That's right, Papa,' said Amelia, laughing up at him. 'They're all so excited at the thought.'

'Well, you tell all the young ladies to wear warm coats, and we'll see if we can't manage a spin around the square.'

It was going to be such fun, Amelia knew it. Cook was already stacking goodies in the pantry, and Edmund had helped Amelia to make paper lanterns to hang up, and streamers from coloured paper, and the orangery was looking so splendid and now Papa was going to come home early from the office and take people on motor-car rides. Amelia wasn't too sure herself how the dancing part would go, but she knew that was what the girls at school expected, so she just hoped they would know how to handle it. It was all going to be so wonderful. The best party ever.

Amelia was so busy imagining it, and breathing slowly to calm the lurching excitement in her tummy, that she didn't notice the anxious glance her mother exchanged with her father over her head.

And even if she had, she would have assumed it had something to do with Edmund, whose cold hadn't seemed to get any better. In fact, it had got worse. Amelia could hear him coughing and spluttering in the night, even though he still had a fire in his room every evening.

Matthew Sweeney

from

THE SNOW VULTURE

The body of the snow bear was waist-high, exactly as Clive had left it before dinner. Glancing at the snow vulture he was almost surprised. He continued tightly packing more snow on. Fortunately, there was plenty. The bear had to be taller, and bigger in every sense, than the vulture.

He slapped snow, almost aggressively, on the bear's shoulders and pressed it down each time, until the shoulders were as padded as an American footballer's. He took great care with the head (and put a brick from the barbecue inside, to punish head-smashers). All the time he worked fast, because the order to come inside could arrive at any moment. He raided the barbecue's charcoal for the nose, the eyes, the mouth, and the insides of the ears. He made, with great patience, the front and back legs and paws, and somehow attached them to the bear's body. The bear was sitting up. It looked so real to Clive that he thought it might amble over to the vulture, club it to the ground and devour it. If only it would.

Clive felt exhausted and, now that he'd finished working, shiveringly cold. He also felt proud, however, of his big fierce-looking bear. Carl would get a shock in the morning. Who knew what he'd see? Wasn't the polar bear known as the king of the Arctic? This snow bear was king of the roof-garden.

Clive turned with a smirk to the snow vulture, which was puny by comparison. It was the first time he'd looked its way for at least half an hour. It was almost with a start he noticed that the vulture seemed to be staring at the bear. Glaring might be a better word – he'd forgotten how evil it looked. He was sure the vulture had turned slightly while he'd been building the bear. At the same time he knew this was impossible. His mind was playing tricks on him. Nevertheless, as he looked from the bear to the vulture his earlier confidence evaporated. The bear might be bigger but the vulture radiated power. It was like a shark beside a whale.

Cold though he was, then, Clive decided he had to stay and guard his snow bear. He thought for a moment about rigging the hammock up and pulling on all the jumpers, trousers, socks he could find, and getting into one sleeping bag inside three others, but he knew he'd never be allowed. He wouldn't even be allowed to sleep inside the glass door at the top of the stairs. What could he do, then?

Well, he would leave the light on. Lights are deterrents to evil. And if he were at all inventive, he could rig up some kind of warning device that would go off if the snow bear was approached. Carl could have done it, easy. But Carl was banished to the bedroom, and, anyway, he would hardly be prepared to help Clive – especially when he realized what it was to do with.

He thought hard, shivering as he did so. It needn't be a very elaborate device. A simple bell tied to a very long piece of string would do. He could tie the end with the bell around the body of the bear, and take the other end of the string all the way down both sets of stairs to his bedroom where it would be tied to his big toe. And, winter or no winter, he'd leave the bedroom window open. That way, no matter how deeply he slept, he'd have two chances of learning about any attack on his snow bear. If he didn't hear, he'd be sure to feel his toe being tugged.

It wasn't perfect. Carl would have worked out some way of hearing directly in the bedroom, under the pillow perhaps. But it was the best Clive could think of.

With a look at the bear, as if to reassure it, Clive headed down the stairs to find a bell and string. He frightened the life out of his mother who was sitting on her own, by the fire, reading a book. She reacted as though he were a burglar, arrived by helicopter.

'Who is it? Who is it?' she said, jumping up and backing for the door.

'Clive! You've been up there all this time! Are you trying to catch pneumonia? Get down to bed at once and be thankful your father's asleep. I don't believe this!'

Clive glanced upstairs and reluctantly headed down to bed. Even inside he was frozen, especially his hands, nose and feet, so why not stay out? As he lay under the duvet with his teeth chattering, he thought of his beautiful, noble snow bear two floors directly above him. He wished houses had transparent floors. He wished he was a whizz-kid with a video camera, able to set up a night-watch. But five minutes after his mother brought him a very welcome hot-water bottle he was asleep.

* * *

It was late morning. Carl had gone to school but Clive was still in bed. Outside the open door of his room his mother was speaking to the doctor.

'I told him not to go up there. I warned him. I knew he'd end up like this.'

The doctor nodded his head with a little smile

that showed he wasn't in the slightest interested. He pushed his glasses back on his nose and handed Clive's mother a prescription.

'Give him one teaspoonful four times a day, and keep him in bed.' He bent down and snapped his black bag shut. Then they both moved out of view towards the door of the flat.

Clive wondered if the doctor knew he'd picked up this dose, not on the roof-garden as his mother believed, but earlier in the school playground when Carl had stuffed snow in his pants. Doctors could tell anything, couldn't they? – anything to do with health. This doctor knew after a few listens on his stethoscope and a few prods on the chest that it wasn't pneumonia Clive had, only a bad dose of cold. He was probably annoyed at being called out for such a trivial matter.

Yet to Clive it didn't feel so trivial. All night long he'd sweated and tossed and turned, and snivelled and sneezed, and now his throat was sore. Just before the doctor came his mother had changed his pyjamas and the sheets on his bed, and the old ones were in the laundry basket, saturated. And behind all the suffering two things were in his mind: that Carl had done this to him; and that he'd left his snow bear on the roof-garden in the company of that snow vulture.

He wanted to do something bad to Carl, something worse than he'd ever done before. The trouble was that he couldn't think what. These things came naturally to Carl. In the area of badness Clive was a beginner.

Then at once he realized the answer was obvious. He'd smash the precious snow vulture. That would annoy Carl more than anything. Clive knew he'd tried to do it before and failed, but he had to get over his ridiculous nervousness towards the vulture. It was only made of snow. It wasn't alive. These were silly ideas Carl was putting in his head.

He thought then of his snow bear and guilt came over him. He hadn't even been up to check it this morning. It could be melted for all he knew. But, to be fair, it wouldn't have been easy for him to get up there. Apart from the fact that his mother had hardly left his room all morning – fussing around like a nurse back from retirement – he'd found his two trips to the toilet excruciatingly difficult, and the toilet was practically next door. He had no energy whatsoever.

He lay back and concentrated, and got his priorities in order. Smashing the snow vulture could wait. He was too weak for such activity. Also, he knew himself it would be dangerous, in his condition, to go out in the snow. But somehow he ought to be able to drag himself up to the door of the roof-garden, and look out to see if his bear was OK.

He decided he had to lie as still as a corpse for as long as possible. No arm or leg movements, no twitches, nothing. That way there would be a build-up of energy in the run-down battery of his body. It would be better than sleeping because his mind would be actively helping him, consciously willing the energy to flow in.

He stared at one spot in the ceiling so long that he half expected it to give way, as if under a blowtorch, and he'd find himself staring at the ceiling of the living-room. He thought of the last book he'd read and liked, one about giants, and he went back in his mind to the start of it, and imagined the story unfolding as a cartoon film on the screen of the ceiling.

Then he must have dozed off because his mother was sitting on his bed, with a bowl of steaming chicken broth on a tray, and was asking him to prop himself up with a pillow so she could feed him.

'I can feed myself,' he said, pulling himself up and realizing he felt much better. Reaching the roof-garden was a definite possibility now.

'How are you feeling, Clive? You look better.' She put her hand on his forehead and nodded.

'Temperature's gone down. Eat this hot soup and feel it working on you. We'll have you up and about in a day or so.'

She left him eating and went to get his

medicine from the fridge. He was enjoying the broth. He hadn't realized, till then, how hungry he'd been. It probably would do him good too.

He decided he had to be a bit careful about his mother. It wouldn't do for her to feel he was too much recovered, else she would be in with his schoolbooks, making him work so he wouldn't fall behind. He didn't want to work.

When he'd swallowed the medicine he told her he felt very weak again, and thirsty. He asked for Lucozade, knowing there was none in.

'I'll be alright on my own till you get back,' he said.

Somewhat to his surprise she agreed to get him some. Sickness seemed to be an advantage in getting favours granted. He must remember that.

While she was getting her coat on he summoned up the tiredest look he could manage, and flopped back on the bed. But no sooner had she closed the door than he was out of bed and in his dressing-gown, and making his way slowly up the stairs.

He had no need to lie about it, he was still very weak. Already at the first landing, under the map of the moon, he had to rest. For a moment he thought about postponing the journey and going back to bed. That would be giving in, however. He struggled on.

Crossing the living-room, which seemed as big

as a field, he had to stop awhile at the first armchair. It was so pleasant, lying back there, that it was a huge effort to get himself on his slippered feet again and moving. Only the knowledge that the supermarket was nearby, and his mother would be back very soon, galvanized him.

He came to the bottom of the last stairs and looked up at the panels of wire-reinforced glass. He gripped the banister tightly and set off, feeling like an arctic explorer at the end of his tether within sight of the North Pole. He took care to avoid the various flowerpots of cacti and Venus fly traps at the side of the stairs. It was a slow climb.

Eventually his head came above the wooden ledge that allowed him the first look at the roof-garden. He gripped the ledge to steady himself. His snow bear was there but, although still recognizable, it bore no comparison to how it had looked the previous evening. It had shrunk to half its size, as if a real bear had been starved for months or had most of its blood and strength sucked out. One end of the brick was poking out of its head.

The vulture was the same as before but now was bigger than the bear. All Clive's remaining energy drained away as he looked at it. He had to hold on extra tight to stop from falling backwards down the stairs. At that moment he heard the door of the flat slam shut as his mother returned from the supermarket.

Martin Waddell

from

LITTLE OBIE AND THE FLOOD

New things take some getting used to, and so do new people.

Marty wasn't new people at Cold Creek, exactly, but she still wasn't someone who had been there before as far as Grandad and Effie were concerned. They didn't know her as well as Little Obie did.

'That girl can't read nor write!' Grandad said. 'I don't know what her Pa was thinking of.'

'You can't neither,' Effie said.

'I can,' Grandad said. 'I can write my name.'

'Is that so?' said Effie.

And later Grandad said, 'That Marty don't eat proper! She picks at her food like a chicken. I guess she needs feeding up.'

'Food don't grow on trees!' said Effie.

'Some does!' said Grandad.

'And some don't!' said Effie.

And another time Grandad said, 'Marty's moping down by the creek again. Some days she don't do nothing but mope. I guess she's missing her Pa.'

'Moping never brought anybody back,' said Effie.

The way Grandad and Effie said things about Marty they sounded hard, but really they were soft inside. They never said a word that would hurt her, because they knew how much she was hurting already.

Little Obie knew it too, but sometimes he couldn't really understand it.

Marty didn't seem like she used to be any more.

'Hey Marty!' Little Obie said. 'Let's go swimming in the Owl Pool.'

'Don't want to go swimming,' Marty said.

'Why not?' asked Little Obie.

Marty didn't say why not. She just went and sat on her own on the old tree trunk by the creek, watching the water.

Little Obie had to go swimming all by himself at the Owl Pool, and he didn't want to do that because he wanted to do things with Marty.

'She's no use – Marty,' Little Obie complained to Effie. 'She won't go swimming, nor nothing.'

'Reckon she's had one swim too many,' said Effie. 'It's no wonder she won't go swimming after what happened to her Pa.'

'Oh,' said Little Obie.

'You be good to her, Little Obie,' said Effie.

'She'll get over it.'

But Marty didn't.

She just sat by the creek gazing at the swirling water, and most times she didn't even seem to hear when Little Obie suggested they should go up to the ridge, or how about a tree climb.

One time, Little Obie came by the creek and Marty told him to go away, and then she started crying, and the next thing she ran off in the woods, and Grandad was cross. Marty didn't come back till almost dusk, and when she did she just went and sat by the fire and never said a thing, but her eyes were all buggy like she'd been crying.

'Is that your doing, Little Obie?' asked Effie, when Marty had gone to bed.

'I didn't do nothing!' Little Obie said. 'I don't *have* to do nothing to set her off. She's not like she used to be – Marty.'

'Marty's been sick,' said Grandad.

'She ain't sick now,' said Little Obie.

'Just sad,' said Grandad. 'That's the way it is, Little Obie. And you and me and Effie just got to bear with it till some of the sadness wears away.'

'Well, I'm fed up with Marty anyway!' said Little Obie.

For a while he didn't talk much to Marty in case she'd start crying or run off and he'd get into trouble. But then he started talking again, because inside he was very fond of Marty and he wanted her to be like she was before the flood, and not like she was after when her Pa was drowned.

Then the hog bit Effie.

It was a bad bite, right in her leg, and Effie had to take to her bed, and she couldn't help Grandad no more.

Grandad was worried. He got out the wagon and he went to the Stinsons and he brought back Mrs Stinson and she did what she could putting Effie to rights, but then she had to see to her own place, and Effie still wasn't right.

Effie got up out of her bed next morning, but she couldn't move much. She just sat in her chair.

'I guess we'll manage,' Grandad said, but he wasn't much good at managing. He hadn't the time for it. He needed to be out in the open, looking after things.

Grandad and Little Obie were cutting down trees for a new barn, to make up for the old one that got washed away. Grandad axed the wood, and Little Obie stripped the branches off, and together they hauled it to where the new barn was going to be.

When they got back to the cabin at noon, everything was going.

There was a good fire lit, and coffee brewing, and Effie sitting there in the chair with her old bitten leg and a smile on her face, which was something strange because Effie didn't smile a lot.

'Reckon somebody just wakened up!' she told Grandad.

There was bacon, cornbread and squash for their meal, and more coffee, and when that was done and they were all sitting about, Marty was still on the move.

Marty looked after the house at Cold Creek like it had never been looked after before, and she looked after Effie too, and kept on doing it until Effie was better and able to move about. Then Marty started in doing the wood with Little Obie and helping Grandad with the hogs and the fencing, and when she ate she didn't pick at her food like a chicken any more, she gobbled like a turkey.

'Where'd you learn your manners, girl?' Grandad said, straight to her face.

'You keep eating, Marty!' Effie said. 'Never mind about manners.'

But when Little Obie and Grandad were down by the creek, Effie showed Marty the way people usually eat, without gobbling, and Marty never minded one bit.

Effie got hold of Little Obie the next morning and sat him down with Marty at the table. Together they started teaching Marty to read and write. Marty wrote her own name: MARTY HANSEN. It was a bit squiggly, but she showed it to Grandad when he came in and he knew who it was.

'You write yours,' she said to Grandad.

'Reckon I'll do it for you some other time,' said Grandad, and he went off.

'I'm going to be a lady, reading and writing!' Marty said proudly. 'Then I'll be real grown up.'

'Don't you be in no hurry to grow up,' said Effie, 'coz you'll grow up just the same!'

Next time Little Obie went off to the Owl Pool for his swim, Marty went with him.

The Owl Pool was great for swimming, because of the deep dark bit, and Little Obie didn't think Marty would go in it, but she did. She never stopped to think about it, she just dove in.

She still went out by the creek sometimes and sat on the log looking at the water, but now Little Obie sat with her. Sometimes they sat and looked and didn't say nothing, and sometimes they chucked sticks and sometimes they talked.

Marty didn't forget about her Pa, she couldn't do that, but she didn't spend all day moping any more. She wasn't the same Marty as before, but she was getting better and beginning to be happy.

'Reckon it's wearing off now,' Little Obie told Effie.

'Reckon so,' said Effie.

'Only she still misses her Pa,' said Little Obie.

'There ain't nothing we can do about that, Little Obie,' said Effie.

Little Obie went off to the creek, all by himself,

and he sat on the log and looked at the water just like Marty did sometimes. He thought and thought about how he could help Marty, but he couldn't think of anything to do except just being there to talk to her when she wanted him.

So that's what he did.

John Quinn

from

THE SUMMER OF LILY AND ESME

It was Tatters' excited barking that woke Alan. He had slept deeply and long. A glance at his watch told him it was ten past ten. It took a few moments for him to become familiar again with his new surroundings. Glebe House. This was his new home. This was his new room. This was – Tatters broke his reverie. He stumbled out of bed and pulled back the curtains. The flood of light drowned him momentarily, but as his eyes became accustomed to the brightness he marvelled at the view before him. Trees and meadows sailed towards him out of receding mist, as a warm May sun broke through.

Down below, Tatters was yapping away at Tom Grehan. Tom leaned across the crossbar of his bicycle and talked softly to the dog. Tatters sat on his haunches a few yards away and barked back but Tom kept talking as if to a child. Tatters finally relented and crawled forward on his belly until Tom could reach down and gently scratch the dog's head. Tatters had made a friend. Tom was still hunched across the crossbar talking to the dog when Alan's father appeared in his dressing-gown and slippers.

The two men conversed for a few minutes, Tom gesturing towards the house now and then while the younger man nodded earnestly. In one of his gestures Tom pointed towards Alan's window and caught sight of the boy's face. Tom waved cheerily and, as Alan returned the wave, he was disappointed to see Tom mount his bike and head off down the avenue with Tatters frisking along behind him. 'Breakfast, Alan,' his mother called, 'and hurry. We have to get to Mass at eleven.'

Mass was in the village of Kildavock, about two miles from Glebe House. Kildavock was a small village, just one street with a supermarket and a few pubs. The church was at the far end of the village. As his father parked the car, Alan was aware of the curious stares of the local people as they hurried in twos and threes into the church. In particular the newcomers came under the gaze of a knot of men at the church gate, men who were in no hurry to go inside. Among them was Tom Grehan, who gave a little salute to the McKay family as they passed by. Kildavock would know all about the newcomers before Mass was over, Alan thought as he dipped his finger in the water font and entered the cool dark of the church.

* * *

'No *Sunday Times*!' Alan's father muttered as he slid into the driving seat, tossing a chocolate bar towards Alan in the back. 'Had to order the damn thing. The joys of living in the wilds.'

'You'll get used to it, dear,' his wife answered. 'There are compensations. Did you talk to Tom?'

'Yes. He and his sidekick, Mick, will follow us over.'

'Oh, good,' Alan cried. 'Will he be with us all day?' The prospect of having a friend around the house for his first day cheered him. His mother's reply dimmed that cheer quickly. 'They're coming to help us with the furniture. Heavy work, not really for boys.'

'But I could –'

'You could change out of your good clothes and bring Tatters for a walk.'

'And keep him out of our way,' his father added. There would be no point in arguing any further. It was Tatters and himself against the world.

Alan changed into a tee-shirt and Bermuda shorts and called Tatters. Although he was disappointed that he could not meet Tom Grehan – and hopefully find out a bit more about the ghost in the attic – it was still nice to get outside.

The day had grown very warm. As he made his

way down the orchard he welcomed the shade of the apple trees. There was a glorious scent from the grass Tom had cut, a scent Alan had never experienced before. He lay down on the grass that had fallen to Tom's scythe and tumbled with Tatters, gathering armfuls of the stuff and covering them both in its delicious scent. Tatters soon tired of the game, however, and was off bounding through the uncut grass in the lower part of the orchard. Alan lay where he was, panting from his exertions and brushing the grass from his body. He threw back his head and lay with arms and legs outstretched. The sun was directly overhead, and it was when he shielded his eyes from its glare with his hand that his gaze fell on the little window high up on the back wall of the house. The attic. It must be the attic. And that must be the window where the ghost – the boy – was seen. There was certainly no face there now. In fact the window was distinctly grimy, unlike the other windows, which glinted in the sunlight.

Alan felt the same chill and thrill that had run through him when Tom had first mentioned the ghost. Tom. Maybe if he hung around he might get a word with Tom before he began work. Maybe if he went down the avenue ...

Tatters' excited barking interrupted his thoughts. Alan jumped up and it was some time before he could actually catch a glimpse of the dog. The grass was so tall that Tatters had to bound through it in kangaroo hops. Alan laughed at the comical sight of the little black-and-white bundle bobbing up and down. But Tatters had obviously disturbed something and there was a chase on. A rabbit? A hare? Alan gave a whoop and joined in, lunging through the tall grass. He too found it difficult to run and ended up hurdling rather than sprinting, often stumbling and falling over concealed hillocks. He laughed each time he picked himself up, thinking how comical *he* must look. Each time he had to listen for Tatters before he could pick up the trail. The chase took boy, dog and quarry in a crazy zig-zag path which gradually brought them to the bottom of the orchard. Alan paused, breathless from the chase.

A huge wall of brambles, twice his height, confronted him. Tatters grew even more excited, frustrated by the barrier that allowed his quarry an escape. He ran along the hedge, seeking a way through. And then, in a moment, he was gone. 'No, Tatters, no,' Alan cried, desperately lunging after the dog towards a small gap in the thicket. The dog had disappeared but Alan's momentum carried him right into the thicket. Instinctively he threw his hands up to protect his face from the brambles. His legs kept going and he landed with a thud on his bottom. Before he had time to recover from the shock of the impact, an amazing thing happened.

Alan careered downwards through the undergrowth, lying on his back. His arms flailed as he fought desperately to protect his face. He willed his body to stop but it would not. For a fleeting moment he had a memory of a similar experience – sliding down water rapids at the seaside leisure park. But this was no joyride. As his feet cleared a path, sally rods whipped the rest of his body viciously as if sprung from traps. The brambles were even worse, tearing at his clothes, tangling his hair and lacerating his arms and legs. He fought for his breath, trying to scream, if only in pain, but no sound came from his throat. Once he caught hold of a thick branch, hoping to stop his mad feet-first slide, but the branch snapped and came away in his hand. He shut his eyes tightly for fear of a whipping bramble. His descent seemed almost vertical, plunging him into a hell of torment. His body gained speed as he descended, so much so that it travelled too fast for the whipping rods to hit him, but still the occasional one lashed him, sending a searing pain right through him. The fall seemed as if it would never end, but just when he feared that an even worse fate might await him at the bottom, he shot out into blinding light and landed in a carpet of soft, soft, beautifully soft grass.

The next sensation Alan felt was that of Tatters' warm, moist tongue licking his torn legs. He must have passed out, for how long he did not know. As sensation returned to his body, so did pain. Stinging pain seared through his arms and legs. Blood oozed from a number of red weals which scarred his limbs. His tee-shirt and shorts were badly torn and bits of briar still dangled from both garments. Tatters' attempts to comfort him only seemed to sharpen his pain.

'It's all your fault anyway,' Alan whimpered, shoving the dog away from him. The sudden movement of doing so only made him more aware of how sore his whole body was. Tatters slunk away, not understanding the boy's change of mood. Alan slowly eased himself into a sitting position and surveyed his damaged body. He gathered wisps of dry grass and gently wiped his wounds. There was nothing he could do about his clothes. He thought of how his mother would react on seeing him. He winced as he dabbed at a particularly deep gash. He winced even more as he thought of his mother's response. When he had cleaned himself as much as he could, he lay back in the long grass and reflected on his situation. The pain was slowly easing from his body. There remained the problem of making his way back to his own garden. The bramble and thicket wall through which he had plunged looked even more daunting from this side. He was on a much lower level now – so much so that he could not see Glebe House. Yet there was something about his fall that bothered him. Yes, there had been a tangle of briars and undergrowth but apart from that the passage through which he slid was quite clear underneath, almost as if ...

Alan suddenly became aware of voices in the distance. He listened intently. Above the drone of insects and occasional birdsong, the sound of human voices carried over the drowsy stillness. Alan rolled over and eased himself into a kneeling position. It brought his head and shoulders above the meadow grass. Across the meadow, beyond a low hedge, he could see the back of a two-storey house. This must have been the house whose roof he had noticed from his own window. It wasn't so much the house that attracted his attention now but the voices of two figures who were seated in a clearing just beyond the hedge. Two women, wearing large straw hats.

From a distance he could make out little else but the excited chatter of the pair and the occasional rattle of a tea-cup carried across the hazy meadow. Alan was about to duck down again and make his retreat when Tatters' barking distracted him once again. That dog! Tatters had appeared at the hedge just beside the two figures. There was nothing for it but to retrieve him as quickly as possible. Alan waded across the meadow. An occasional thistle brushed against his legs, reminding him how sore they were. He reached the hedge, called to Tatters in a whisper, grabbed him and swept him into his arms. He didn't dare look across the hedge, and turned to make his escape.

'There you are, Albert. Where ever have you been these last few days?' The voice was frail, and though it seemed to be directed at him, Alan didn't turn around. It couldn't be.

'Yes, Albert, we've been watching out for you every day.' It was a different voice, slightly stronger. He turned to face them, the dog still squirming under his arm. They were old, very old. He could barely see their faces under the straw hats. One of the women sat upright in a wheelchair, the other reclined in a sun-chair with a walking-stick propped against it.

'I'm – I'm sorry – I'm not – the dog,' Alan stuttered.

'Oh, we don't mind Ruffian, do we, Lily?' the woman in the wheelchair replied.

'Just keep him away from Tickles,' added Lily.

'Tickles?' queried Alan.

'Yes, Tickles – our cat. Really, Albert, you're ...'

'Albert!' Esme interrupted her sister. 'What on earth happened to you?' She peered out from under her hat and began to giggle. 'Look, Lily! Albert's fallen down the chute – again!'

Lily joined in the giggling. This is crazy, Alan thought. They are crazy. The chute – what did they mean?

'Look, I'm afraid I'm not who you think I am. I'm sorry. I must ...'

'So you should be too,' said Lily, changing her tone. 'You might at least have said if you enjoyed the book.'

'Yes,' added Esme. 'What are we going to tell Father?'

Father, Alan thought. They were positively ancient. How could their father be ...

'Next time he writes from the front he'll say, 'Did Albert enjoy the book?''

The front? That means a war?

'And we'll say,' chimed in Lily, 'oh, yes. He loved it so much he never came back for a week!' They were really ganging up on him now.

'No, I didn't,' Alan pleaded. 'I mean, I wasn't – I'm not –' This was mad. Why am I defending myself? Why can't I explain? I must get out of here.

'Oh, come on, Albert,' Esme laughed. 'Don't sulk! We're only teasing.'

'I'm not sulking,' Alan said. 'I'm only trying to explain.'

'You don't have to explain,' Lily reassured him. 'We know why. Your father wouldn't let you come. And now you stole out and fell down the chute!'

'Again,' added Esme, and they both exploded into giggles once more. This is too much, Alan thought. 'I have to go,' he blurted. 'I'll – I'll come back – soon!' He turned and ran through the meadow, still holding Tatters. He could hear their giggles receding behind him as he ran. He reached the bramble wall, released Tatters and paused for breath. The last hour had been a nightmare. Was it real? Had it happened to him? Maybe it was a case of 'Alan in Wonderland'? He managed a smile to himself.

There was still the problem of getting back to his own garden. He crouched, made himself as small as he could and began the painful climb back up the – the chute! This was the chute! But who was Albert? And who were those doddery old women who talked of a father who was still in the war? The questions raced through his mind, now and then clashing with the painful memory of his descent down the chute as he became entangled in another briar. Progress was slow. He slipped back a number of times, colliding with Tatters who struggled behind him. Eventually he made it to the top, stood up with relief, brushed himself off and headed for the house. He was surely for it now. He took a deep breath, opened the back door and stepped inside.

Eugene McCabe

from

CYRIL: THE QUEST OF AN ORPHANED SQUIRREL

It was almost dawn. Late September. Though half asleep in his drey, Cyril could sense the approach of day. He could tell from two things – the angle of the light and the clamour of nearby crows. At first glimmer they would begin their raucous cawing, and most mornings two young ones would come gliding over to perch above him, joking and mocking.

He could hear them now as they flapped from branch to branch, taunting him:

> 'Little Cyril lives up high,
> Alone, alone; we hear him cry.'

Unkind neighbours, Cyril thought. More than that – cruel, really.

For, last October his parents had left the beech wood at Drumard and gone to the townland of Knockballymore where there were magnificent oak trees laden with acorns. Cyril had been too small to travel. They had not returned. Two days passed, then four, then six, then one week, two weeks, three weeks, and then the leaves had turned from green to yellow, brown and gold. Suddenly it was November. In three days almost every leaf had gone and Cyril was alone in the great bare crown of beech, staring across Burdantien Lough and Summerhill Lough to the Dummy's Lough, and beyond that to the beautiful lough of Knockballymore, through the sky-drenching rains, with cold, dark winds from the west.

In the ten townlands round about there was no other family of red squirrels. Cyril was an orphan. The winter had been long, hard, lonely; the summer busy; and now almost a whole year had passed and it was September again – early Lammas floods spilling over lake and river bottom lands; cattle, hockdeep, plodding to higher ground; swallows in their hundreds on telephone lines, aware of the coming darkness and dreaming of the light of Africa. Soon they would be gone. Where could he go? Would he have to spend another winter here with no company but cold lakes and bare drumlins?

He opened his eyes and looked out over the top of his grass-lined drey. Through the lower escape hatch he could see the greeny-grey lichen on the beech trunks, and the floor of the wood scattered with brown and yellow leaves.

'Little Cyril lives up high,
Alone, alone; we hear him cry.'

Young crows were very foolish, Cyril thought.
They wanted him to suddenly leap from his nest
and jump at them. They liked to be frightened.

He stretched the forefingers on each of his paws
and moved his thumbs, then straightened his five
sharp toes. Slowly, he uncurled his long, round,
bushy tail. It was glossy, and the colour of dark
copper. He crept to the escape hatch. The two young
crows were above him. They did not see him come
out. Crouching in the fork of a branch under his nest
he could hear them chattering and mocking.

'If he's all that lonely why stay here?'

'He's lazy, that's why. Asleep all winter. Then all
summer plundering and storing.'

Cyril could not see them yet. He knew from the
sound exactly where they were sitting. He crept out
on a branch, filled his lungs with air, then shot,
feet spread, across a high open space, curled his
tail around a branch and slung his body up ten feet,
sailing between the two crows, who fell, flapping
with sudden, laughing squawks. Blinking, he
watched as they cackled insults. They hated
squirrels. Strange, he thought, how creatures who
lived by thieving and plundering were so quick to
condemn the same things in others. He watched
them float down towards the house – a white,
four-square house with a basement.

In the beech wood where Cyril lived there were about a hundred trees, some over two hundred years old. Behind the house there was a square yard of stone outbuildings, and behind that a kitchen garden with seven apple trees, two plum trees and one pear tree. There were other delights – loganberries, strawberries, blackberries, gooseberries, and raspberries. It was the apples he liked best. Sometimes he split them and ate the seeds.

He was thinking of nipping down for an apple when, away to his right, high in the beech trees, there was a great commotion among the crows. Cyril watched, trying to hear what the argument was about. He knew a little crow language. There seemed to be about six warning words: watch, gun, food, man, cat, death. He had heard all these words until he was tired hearing them. But what he had never heard before was all the crows cawing the word 'death' together. This, now, was the only word that seemed to emerge from the argument. Then he saw eight crow cocks in a circle, and in the middle an old crow.

For weeks, Cyril had watched the old crow. Ten trees away he sat in a high branch, night and day, staring at the countryside. He had a damaged wing and was blind in one eye. Now and then the other crows swooped around him, mocking his age and defects. When they did this the old crow sat perfectly still and silent.

Now they were all around him, cackling loudly. Then there was a sudden silence. One by one the eight crows nodded at each other. Suddenly they jumped on the old crow, and then all fell, flapping and squawking to the ground, pecking without mercy. In less than half a minute the eight flew up and left the old, blind crow lying dead. A tabby cat came padding out from the yard and walked off with the dead crow.

Cyril was shocked. He stared down at the spot where the crow had lain. He shivered in fear and felt more lonely than ever. He longed to have someone who could explain things.

He thought of his friend Charlie, the badger. Charlie had told him about crow courts, but he had never seen one until now. To be killed by your own sort for some misdeed, defect, or for old age must be the most awful way to die, Cyril thought.

In the silence that followed the killing, Cyril sat, blinking gloomily. The crows were quiet. The sun had come out, the lake was a blinding shield, and somewhere a chainsaw began its hard, low moan as it clawed its way through the butt of a tree. No point in sitting on an old plough, brooding and feeling sad, Cyril thought. I'll go to Charlie. He thought again of the lonely winter ahead. How could he face that? Maybe Charlie would have some suggestions.

Janet McNeill

from

WE THREE KINGS

The school was built on a hillside a little distance from the town. The road down to the sea-front passed the field where Big Joe kept his donkeys when the season was over. The big barn in the field gave the animals cover during the worst of the winter. They were social beasts and missed the stir and bustle of the beach. Now they pushed their rough necks across the gate, snuffling goodwill. Dan rubbed their noses.

Now his route took him along the sea-front. This afternoon it was almost deserted. This was the way he liked it. The sea sounded wild and sad, not the tame water in which holiday makers swam and squealed and children trailed their boats. The tide was coming up the sand fast, green glass turned to lace as each wave tipped over.

A couple of months ago this sand would have been packed tight with deck chairs, sprinkled all over with picnic parties, studded with castles and scarred with moats and the tracks of the donkeys, strewn with paper bags, orange peel, lollipop sticks. Now, except for the zigzag of seagulls' feet the beach was as unmarked as it had been when this morning's outgoing tide had uncovered it. The brown festoons of seaweed lay where the water had dropped them.

Because the sky was overcast the daylight had already begun to fade, and in a few of the houses the lights were lit. At this time of year these were the honest lights of home, not the crazy confusion of red and green and blue that winked and spun on summer evenings, spelling out the ways in which the visitors could spend their money. The awnings in front of the shops had been taken down and stored, the racks of postcards and toys no longer stood on the pavement, inviting customers. The boating lake was deserted except for the plastic gnomes and storks, the amusement arcade was silent, no chance for the last coin in your pocket to make a millionaire of you. Two of the chip shops were shuttered, and no table-cloths gleamed through the boarding-house windows. The exhausted landladies had waved good-bye to the last of their guests and had taken themselves off on their own holidays.

Dan liked this feeling of emptiness. He could smell the sea, unmixed with any whiff of hot dogs or chips. A solitary gull idled a few feet above his head, crying mournfully, and he loved it. Already some of the lights were lit in the big Hotel at the further end of the bay. A couple of dozen wealthy people stayed there throughout the winter, when the bus tours had dried up. It was because of her work at the Hotel that the hoover had been busy at home the evening Dan was practising his Shakespeare. Mum was catching up. She was always catching up, as if she proved something to herself by being twice as busy since Dan's father had come to a full stop.

A car drew in smoothly at Dan's elbow, cleverly matching its pace with his own. Uncle Bill on his way home from his office in the city. The building trade was booming. The car was this year's model. Uncle Bill had built himself a fine house at the far end of the town. 'The air out there's lovely,' Aunt Florence was fond of telling Mum.

'Hiya!'

Dan said, 'Oh. Hallo.'

'Hop in!' Uncle Bill commanded, large and smiling like he always was. 'I'll take you as far as your corner.'

Dan obeyed, determined not to be impressed, not to sink too deeply into these impossibly soft seats.

'Late this evening, aren't you?'

'There was a meeting after school.'

'They work you hard at that place,' Uncle Bill

suggested, 'but I daresay you keep up all right. Hard work never hurt anyone, you don't get far in this world without it, that's what I tell Roger. He's on the road, is he?'

'I think he stayed to talk to someone.' Let Roger explain for himself what business he had with those kids.

'Always plenty to say for himself, our Roger,' Uncle Bill agreed. He stopped the car at the corner to allow Dan to get out. 'And tell your father to drop in any time he's around. Always a welcome on the mat, tell him that!'

Dan slammed the door of the car a little more vigorously than Uncle Bill would have liked, and turned towards home.

This was the corner where the steepest road from the upland countryside joined the sea-front. Dan wondered if he would ever go past it now without remembering. It was a bad corner. It had been known to be a bad corner, accidents had happened there before the June evening three months ago when Megan's young brother Philip had come careering down the hill, whooping and swooping, on his bicycle. The long hill was a favourite challenge for boys and their bicycles, they knew every twist and trick of the descent, they knew how long it was possible to come at full speed, and which was the last moment when brakes must be eased in, and the flying hedges pulled to an easy pace.

Philip Lloyd had let that last moment go by. He had crashed at full speed into the sea wall and was unconscious when the ambulance reached him. It would be a long job, they said at the hospital, it was possible he might learn to walk again. The machine was so battered that it had been impossible to establish the state of the brakes. The local newspaper suggested that the sun might have been in the boy's eyes, and added a recommendation that youngsters' bicycles should be overhauled at regular intervals.

Dan knew that at the time of the accident the evening sun at this corner couldn't have dazzled a cyclist's eyes. He also knew that Philip's bicycle had been in his father's shop for an overhaul at the beginning of the week. Everyone in the town knew this too.

As he went past the telephone booths Dan found he was treading on broken glass. So the Wreckers had been at it again. The Wreckers, that was the name the town had given to the gang, whoever they were, who had been active all year. Street signs were broken, awnings slashed, window boxes uprooted, you name it, they wrecked it. The local police hadn't a chance against these wily workers of destruction. This time it had been the turn of the telephone booths.

Now Dan had reached his father's shop. He went

past it quickly, telling himself that he knew there wouldn't be any light in the window or any sight or sound of activity, so that he could dodge the sick feeling he got in his stomach if he forgot to be prepared for disappointment. He used to enjoy dropping into the shop on his way home from school, smelling the sharp smell of newly-cut timber, of paint or enamel, as he opened the door and stood without speaking until his father looked up from whatever work absorbed him and saw that Dan was there.

Of course there was no light in the workshop tonight. He was nearly home now. Home was the end house of the tall old-fashioned terrace of houses beside the railway bridge, just before the railway entered the station. One wall of the house was built right against the bridge. Dan's bedroom was on this side. Whenever a train crossed the bridge his room shivered, as if the train picked up the little house in its teeth and shook it gently before it set it down again. Dan liked to be awake in the early morning when the newspaper-and-milk train arrived. The square of light reflected from his bedroom mirror trembled against the wallpaper and sometimes the windowpane rattled.

'Late tonight, aren't you? And mind the floor, I've just done it over.' Mum was knitting and working at the crossword while she waited for the washing machine to complete its final spin.

'Hallo, Dad.'

'Hallo.' Dad didn't turn away from the television. His hands were white now, even the thumbs.

'I was just saying to your father he ought to take a turn along the road to meet you, a breath of fresh air always does you good, doesn't it, Dad?'

'That's right.'

Mum said, 'You don't really want this rubbish on, do you, Dad?' and got up to turn the television off. 'Mind what you're doing with that cigarette ash,' she told him.

'Well, what kept you late?' she wanted to know, and Dan told her about Mr Bingham's list and the Nativity Play.

'A Nativity Play?'

'Joe was hoping it would be Robin Hood or a Pantomime.'

His father hadn't looked at him or smiled. He must make what he was saying matter to Dad.

'Remember the time we went to the Panto, Dad? A couple of years ago?'

'Of course he remembers, don't you, Dad?' Mum supplied.

'It was just Dad and me. You were out with Aunt Florence. You remember the clowns, Dad? The big one who put the little one into the waste paper basket? You must remember!' They had laughed themselves sore over that clown, all the way home they had laughed.

'Your Dad told me about it afterwards. Of course he remembers,' Mum repeated. 'This Nativity Play – you're in it, are you?'

'Yes.'

'Did you hear that, Dad? Dan's in the school play. What part are you doing?'

'I'm to be one of the Three Kings.'

'Well now! Which one? First King, are you?'

Here we go again. 'I don't know about First. I'm King Melchior, Mr Bingham said.'

His mother sniffed. 'Oh – Melchior – he's the old one.' Mum knew a lot about things like that, between her crosswords and having been at Sunday School when she was little.

'I didn't know Melchior was old.'

'Who's to be Caspar?'

'That's Roger. What's Caspar like?'

'He's the one who leads and brings gold.' He would be, Dan thought sourly.

'And Sid is Baltazar.'

'Well, he would have to be, wouldn't he? And it saves some other lad having to get his face blacked.'

'Sid's all right, Mum.'

'I didn't say he wasn't, did I? Did you hear that, Dad? Roger and Dan are to be Kings. Roger is the First King, the one who leads and brings gold.'

'Why Roger?' Dad asked.

'It's Mr Bingham who chooses.'

His mother asked about the other parts and he told her. 'Megan?' she puzzled when he said who had been chosen for Mary.

'Everyone thought it should have been Annette.'

'Did you hear that, Dad? Dan says Megan Lloyd's chosen to be Mary.'

Of course Dad had heard. Megan Lloyd, Philip's sister, Mum didn't have to spell it out like that. The Lloyd family was the last thing Dad would want to talk about. Not that anything seemed to mean very much to him now. If he heard what she said he agreed with it. If he didn't hear, his silence made no difference to her.

Dan ached for things to be the way they used to be at home, easy and ordinary, not this terrible, careful politeness. Big Joe, who lived with his wife and family in a caravan in the field full of donkeys, argued with Mrs Joe. He shouted at her. She shouted at him. You heard them hard at it when you were going past. In the evening you saw them going out to The Holly Tree, Mrs Joe all dolled up and both as happy as Larry.

There must be some way of making Dad take notice of something. You couldn't let what had happened wipe out the whole history and language and pattern of a family. Maybe the sun had after all jumped across the sky and dazzled Philip Lloyd's eyes. Of course Dad remembered those clowns.

'Everyone is to be asked to help, Dad, Mr Bingham said so. People who aren't in the play will be in the choir or playing their recorders. Miss Hunt and the Art Department are doing the costumes and the scenery. Anyone in the town who can help will be helping.' He drew a deep breath. 'I told Mr Bingham you would make the crooks for the shepherds.'

Neither Dad nor Mum spoke. For once Mum was waiting for Dad to speak first. Go on – say something.

'Mr Bingham said he knew you would make a good job of them, Dad.' Dan added.

There was no noise in the room except the dry rasp of his father's hands.

'Well of course he'll make a good job of it, won't you, Dad?' Mum said at last. 'Anything your father does he makes a good job of it.'

Dan knew there was one more thing he could say and he said it. 'When Mr Bingham said Dad would make a good job of the crooks for the shepherds Roger seemed to think it was funny.'

Meta Mayne Reid

from

THE TWO REBELS

PROLOGUE
April 1798

It was on an April evening 1798 that the twins,
Bess and Andrew McIlroy, saw where the long,
keen-edged pike was hidden at Greenan.

The farm lay in the throat of a glen running east
to west in the Londonderry hills. It overlooked a
bustling little river, rich in trout, and on the far
bank of this stood the oldest man-made thing on
the farm – the Giant's Cradle, a ruined Stone-age
fort which still contained an underground hiding
place which Cousin Barney called a souterrain. The
twins called it a 'hidey-hole', and it could be very
useful if they wished to disappear for an hour or
two. On the eastern boundary of the farm was
tumbled moorland where footpads sometimes lay
in wait for farmers coming from the fair in

Lisnamillen. To the west, lay Clonmany sand hills and a wide sea lough.

Foreign news came in this way: of America, where even the stupidest lad could make a fortune, and of the Revolution in France almost ten years before. Now all the talk was of Napoleon Bonaparte's plans to invade the south of Ireland, bringing help to Irish patriots. The Irish news usually came from the east, and at present it was about the United Irishmen who were plotting in Belfast and Antrim and Ballynahinch to overthrow the Irish Government, which was in fact responsible to England and controlled mainly by men who knew little and cared less about conditions in Ireland. This Government, said the United Irishmen, would be replaced by one which would treat men of all classes and creeds alike – as the best of the French revolutionaries had hoped in the days when they shouted for 'Liberty, Equality and Brotherhood.'

Such news and talk were only whispered. Many sympathised but dared not risk hanging, or transportation, or gaol without trial.

Bess and Andrew, being the two eldest children, knew many of the rumours, for often Papa lost temper and discretion together, and talked wildly to Mama, saying that a man might as well be out with the United Irishmen fighting for the poor against the rich as slaving on a farm for a silly wife and five children. At the moment, the five-year-old and the four-year-old were with kindly Aunt Meg at Clonmany, recovering from the chincough, and Greenan only housed the whining sickly baby, and the twins.

They were glad that the younger children were away, for now they had more time to do as they pleased, and to talk about chancy subjects such as rebellion, and of other matters about which they were supposed to be ignorant, such as the case of James Rourke in Coolavaddy, who had refused to allow his house to be searched for arms. Andrew saw him hunted by soldiers through the streets, cornered and lashed until he fell senseless.

Bess had not seen that, but she could not forget poor old Cissy Boyle shivering among her sticks of furniture in the wintry rain outside the cottage from which she had been evicted – because for the second time in thirty years she could not pay the rent punctually. 'What will become of me?' she wailed. 'Where'll I go, where'll I lay my head tonight?' Bess gave her the only penny she had, and, as neighbours gathered round, ran home in tears. Suppose Papa could not pay his dues, and they too were driven from their home to wander as beggars on the roads? It was very frightening. If you were rich and well-born and went to the Episcopal Church, all was well, but if you were poor and a Dissenter, no one cared what happened to you. As Papa said: 'They get the heart of the loaf and we get the dirty crust.'

The only person in the world with whom the twins could discuss these things was Uncle James. They thought of him as an elder brother, for he was only twenty, just eight years older than they. Even if he made friends with the strangest people, and did wild things, he always had time for the twins and stood between them and punishment. They loved James.

On this evening in April they were lying in their favourite place among the hay in the stable loft. They had made a tunnel next to the wall so that they could either look through the cobwebby window in the gable, or through a veil of hay into the stable itself. Now, with Bess's dark curls near Andrew's fair head, they talked in whispers of what they would do when they grew up, for of course they would be together then as they were now. Andrew would study law and perhaps go into Parliament (Mama's cousin, Mr Barney Tulip, had put this notion into his head, for he was a good and respected lawyer in Coolavaddy, some four miles away and had advised on Andrew's schooling). Once Andrew was making a living he would send for Bess to be his housekeeper, and they would make the Grand Tour together '... and see Boney's Palace, and the guillotine, and ...'

'Hush,' said Bess. 'I hear someone.'

Below them in the meadow, Tinker the pony whickered, and through the April dusk came two young men, with Punch, the black-and-white sheepdog, at their heels.

The lad who moved springily as a dancer was Uncle James, easily distinguished by his flaming red hair. The other's dark locks fitted close as a cap, and between black lashes his eyes were startlingly blue (Bess knew this, though Andrew had not noted the fact). All his movements were quick and eager, as if he were trying to hurry on events to suit himself. The twins had only seen him twice before: once on horseback, clearing a high gate near the ford, and once when Lady Charlotte de Courcy's carriage broke down on its way to a ball in Coolavaddy Assembly Rooms. He was Hugh Thomas Fitzhugh, younger son of Sir Thomas Fitzhugh of Castledhu, whose crest was a flaming torch with the words below 'I shall defend.' The Fitzhughs moved in a very different world from struggling farmers such as the McIlroys, and the twins had not realised that Uncle James even knew him, yet as they watched he clapped James on the back. 'You're too cautious by half, James. None's here but the pony and Punch.'

'Indeed, sir, you'll be safe enough at Greenan.'

'Sir?' The voice with its hint of English accent carried clear from the meadow to the listeners in the barn. 'Sir? Aren't we all brothers in the United

Irishmen? You must believe that I wish you to call me Hugh, and de Courcy John, as we call you James.'

Uncle's voice sounded like thick country broth after foreign wine, thought Bess, as he answered, 'As you will, but it's hard to get off my tongue – Hugh.'

'Then I hope you find your pike drill easier.'

'Ay, I mind that well enough.'

'And your catechism?'

Mystified the twins looked at each other: Catechism? This was not a church. But the two young men were already repeating, questions and responses so swift that the children could hardly make sense of them.

'What are you first?'

'A citizen of the world.'

'What are you second?'

'An Irishman among his equals.'

'What are you next?'

'Wronged.'

'Where are you going?'

'To right that wrong.'

'How will you right it?'

'By my own hand.'

'Who goes with you?'

'My brothers.'

'Who are they?'

'Lovers of freedom.'

And, 'All men,' said the clear voice. 'All men.'
Bess did not know why, but tears stood in her eyes.
She would have given anything to be a man and to
stand beside the speaker. 'All who wish to see men
given equal rights to vote and worship and take
what calling they will – tenants and landlords,
Papists and Presbyterians, farmers and tradesmen,
English and Irish – and French too if they will help
to make a new Ireland out of our sorry vassal state.
We can no longer be treated as a foundling child.
We must stand on our own feet and make our own
laws.' He smiled and added in a lower tone, 'We
even have the right to make our own mistakes.'

'I'm wishing it was now,' said Uncle James. 'It's
the waiting I hate. If I might use the pike soon –'

'Where is it?'

'Where no one will cast eyes on it in a hurry.' He
came towards the stable, the pony at his heels.
'Away you!' He slapped the creature gently, and
under cover of the little to-do the twins wriggled
down their tunnel and peered through the wisps of
straw into the stable. Uncle James came in,
hoisted himself up on to the empty manger and felt
behind the slightly tilted edge of the roof beam.
Swallows often nested there, and no one ever
disturbed the luck-bringing birds. When he sprang
down a tall pike was in his hand, its head glistening
sullenly in the evening light.

'Ah-h.'

'She'll sort them,' said Uncle James, and felt the edge tenderly.

The twins caught their breaths. Bess felt for Andrew's hand and found it cold as her own. So the United Irishmen were real after all. The half-secret band who wished to take by force what Parliament would not grant by law was here on the very threshold of their home.

Below them the pike flashed once more before it was put back in its hiding place. The young gentleman went quietly back towards the river, his farmer friend strode whistling into the house.

Walter Macken

from

FLIGHT OF THE DOVES

U ncle Toby rose and put on his bowler hat and walked firmly to the door. He turned there.

'Watch your behaviour, boy,' he said. 'I don't have to hold on to either of you. There are schools and places where you can be put. Don't forget that. And don't think I wouldn't put you there.'

On this note he departed, and Finn allowed the muscles of his stomach to relax.

Now, he thought, with a bit of luck, it will be a good long time before we see Uncle Toby again.

He looked across at Derval. She was crying silently. He always found it was better to be gruff with her when she was crying.

'Derval,' he said, 'please stop crying and dry your eyes. I have something to say to you.'

He watched her. She made a great effort. She raised the hem of her dress and wiped her eyes. Then she looked at him.

'Now, Finn,' she said.

'We are going to run away,' he said.

Her eyes widened.

'Where?'

'You don't remember the time Mammy and Daddy brought us on a holiday to see our grandmother. You were too young.'

'It was on a boat,' she said.

'You remember that?'

'That's all,' she said.

'It's enough,' he said. 'Now listen. You go upstairs and take all the books out of your schoolbag and put in all your clothes from the drawer into the bag. Can you do that?'

'Oh, yes.' she said. 'This will be an adventure.'

'Yes,' he said. 'We want to be gone by the time Uncle Toby comes home. He won't know until the morning that we are gone.'

'Oh,' she said. 'Will he chase us?'

'I don't know,' said Finn. 'Maybe he will say good riddance to bad rubbish.'

'If he catches us, will he put us into that old school?' she asked.

'No,' said Finn grimly. 'Nobody will separate us. I don't know how, but they won't.'

'Will I go and do it now, so?' she asked, rising from the chair.

'Do,' said Finn. 'Good girl. I'll tidy up down here.'

She ran up the stairs.

He cleared the delft from the table and put them into the sink and ran hot water on them. The details of what he was going to do were clear in his mind, but the actual carrying out of them was a bit hazy. Once they got on the way, it would unfold, he felt sure, like one of his mother's stories that she made up as she went along.

He had the dishes washed and dried when Derval came down the stairs with her schoolbag. She had it stuffed with clothes.

'Is that good?' she asked.

He examined it. 'We can get more into it,' he said. He went up the stairs with her again. There were two bedrooms up there. The big one where Uncle Toby slept and the back one where he and Derval slept in two bunks, one on top of the other. Her clothes were in nursery drawers, painted blue with small coloured teddy-bears painted on them. She had created some confusion pulling things out. He went through them all again. He discarded some things, and packed in other things.

'Can I bring my teddy?' she asked. This tattered teddy was on her pillow. She had had it for many years. It was hardly distinguishable as a teddy now, lacking one eye, and some stuffing in the left leg. He was going to discard it, but he relented at the look in her eyes.

'All right,' he said, 'but just that. You can carry it. Now dress yourself in these slacks, and put on all

the jerseys you have, one over another, because it
will be cold where we are going. Will you do that?'

'Yes,' she said.

He went downstairs again and he got the coal
for the stove, broke the sticks for it, swept up the
kitchen, and laid the table for the breakfast. He
would have liked to have left all the dirty dishes for
Toby, but if he saw them he might go into their
room to upbraid them. Everything must look the
same as usual.

Then he got his big schoolbag and emptied it
out. He discarded all the books, except one, a
geography book with coloured maps of all the
countries in the world in it. He took the lot of them
upstairs again. Derval was in the room, cocooned
in clothes, so that she could hardly move. He had
to laugh at the sight of her.

'Am I all right?' she asked.

'You are,' he said. 'You will need all those
clothes. But we'll take some of them off now, and
you go and lie down and sleep, because I don't
think we'll get much sleep tonight.'

'I'll never sleep,' she said. 'I know I won't.'

'You'll have to try,' he said.

He took some of the outer garments from her
and then helped her into the top bunk. He pulled
the blankets over her. She lay down looking at him
with one hand under her face.

'Will we have to go across the sea?' she asked.

'We will,' he said.

'In a big boat?' she asked.

'That's right,' he said.

'With money?' she asked. 'I have elevenpence halfpenny in my box.'

His heart sank.

'That should do fine,' he said. 'I have some money too. Will you try and go to sleep now, and dream about the sea and the boat?'

'Will the boat be windy?' she asked.

He listened. When there was high wind it whistled around this terrace of houses and rattled the windows in their frames.

'No,' he said. 'It won't be windy.'

'You will be with me all the time?' she asked.

'I will,' he said.

'I don't mind so,' she said, and almost at once fell asleep. One second she was wide awake and the next she was fast asleep.

He sat on a chair and thought. What he was going to do seemed utterly impossible. He would have to get himself and his little sister on to a big ship, without money, sail across the Irish Sea and then find a grandmother whose address he did not know. All he knew of her was that dim visit some years ago when he was so small that he could hardly remember a thing about it now. Even when he looked at his diary. He got it out again. It was a small one and he had just learned to write at the time, and he had covered each page with huge letters so there was barely room for more than two or three sentences.

Saturday. We are going on a big boat across the sea.

That was the entry for a full page.

Sunday. We crossed the sea on a big boat.

That was another entry. You stupid boy, he thought, why didn't you give more information? Well, it was the first stage anyhow. He got the tin money box from his own drawer and counted the money in it. Nearly all coppers with a few sixpences. Seven shillings and tenpence. With Derval's elevenpence halfpenny, they wouldn't get very far, but it was better than nothing. He thought some more, then, looking at the sleeping girl, he took his air-rifle which was nearly new and his roller skates and he crept out of the room, down into the kitchen and out into the street. It was a long long street of small two-storey houses. It was getting dark. Grey clouds were piling overhead. It would soon rain. He didn't mind that.

Joss lived near the end of the street. He just opened the door and pushed in his head and called, 'Joss!'

'He can't go,' his mother said. 'He hasn't his lessons done.'

'Ah, Mother,' said Joss.

'Only a minute, Mrs Bleaker,' said Finn.

'Mark your minute,' she said, 'or I'll have to beat Joss.'

This was a joke. She wouldn't lay a finger on him.

'I won't be long,' said Joss. He came out.

'Look,' said Finn, holding out the gun and the skates. 'You want those?'

'Boy!' said Joss, eyes gleaming.

'Will you buy them?' Finn asked.

'How much?' asked Joss.

'How much have you got?' Finn asked.

Joss's face fell. 'Not a lot,' he said.

'Go and find out,' said Finn.

Joss went away. Finn kept looking around him, hopping from foot to foot. He felt as if he was being pursued already.

Joss came back. He had money in his hand.

'Ah, it's not enough,' he said. 'Eight and fivepence and a jack knife, that's all.'

'Here you are,' said Finn, handing over the gun and the skates.

'But it's not enough,' said Joss.

'It's enough for now,' said Finn, taking the money and the knife. 'I haven't got a knife.'

'It's a real good one,' said Joss. 'It'll do anything. There's even a spike for taking stones out of horses' hooves.'

'That'll be useful,' said Finn, laughing.

'You never know,' said Joss, hurt. 'Are they really mine?'

'They are,' said Finn. 'I must go now.'

'What's your hurry?' said Joss. 'Can't we play with the gun?'

'There are no pellets,' said Finn. 'You'll have to get pellets.'

'Oh,' said Joss. 'All right. I'll see you tomorrow, then.'

'That's the ticket,' said Finn, already moving away.

'What made you do it?' Joss called after him.

'I knew you wanted them,' Finn called back.

'All right, Santa Claus,' said Joss in disbelief, and then started rubbing the butt of the gun with the palm of his hand.

Finn slowed his running. He didn't want to attract attention. Not that there were many people about, but he was already being cautious. He heard questions in his head: When was the last time the boy and girl were seen? Where were they heading for? What were they wearing?

He went to look at Derval first. She was still sleeping.

He started laying out his own clothes. The best way to carry clothes was on your back, he decided. He had two suits, the everyday one with the short pants and the school blazer, and one for Sundays.

He had several shirts and jerseys. Some of those he could wear. He had a pair of long jeans. They could go over his shorts. Because he needed the bag for other things than clothes.

He went down to the kitchen again. He looked in the larder. There was cold meat there on the bone. He sliced some of this off, but not too much because Uncle Toby always made meat sandwiches for himself when he came home. He took some butter, and he put on a pot and put some eggs into it to hardboil them. He didn't take much bread or all the fruit. He wanted things to look normal if Uncle Toby carried out an inspection. He packed all those things neatly in the bag.

He went upstairs again. It was quite dark in the room now. He knew they would have to be out of the house before Uncle Toby returned, but he didn't want to go until the last minute so that Derval would have plenty of sleep. Otherwise she wouldn't know what was happening to her. Not that she knew much now. He didn't know himself, just that the time had come to get away from Uncle Toby.

He heard the big clock below in the kitchen striking the hours and when it beat out nine o'clock, he started to dress himself, or rather overdress himself. He made sure of the diary that he had it in an inside pocket where he wouldn't lose it. He made sure of the money, and then when he had everything ready he shook Derval.

He had to do a lot of shaking to get her to wake up. When he finally got her awake she looked bewildered and frightened, but then when she recognized him the fright cleared from her face.

'We are going to go now, Derval,' he said.

'Oh,' she said.

'We will dress you up again in all your clothes,' he said. 'You look like a small bear.'

She smiled.

He helped her from the bunk, and helped her to put on her extra clothes. She was bulky, but she would need them all.

'All right now?' he asked. She nodded.

'We'll go,' he said.

He put out the light in the room, and they went downstairs. He put her schoolbag over her shoulder and did the same with his. Hers was light, so it would be no great burden on her.

They stood at the kitchen door and he looked at it. One time it was a happy place, he remembered. It was a great pleasure to come home to it. But all the light of laughter was gone out of it since Toby had taken over the power. It was only a place of fear. He was holding Derval's hand. He switched off the light and they went into the street. There was a miserable drizzle falling, but it suited him. They set off to the right. They turned the corner. There was light in the Red Dragon. The windows were misted. He didn't feel safe until they were past it and heading towards the station.

They would have to be hidden in the station before the loaded boat train arrived from London. It was easy to get in when there were no trains. And once all the people were milling about in the early hours of the morning, two children would not be noticed.

They crossed the street towards the station.

Patricia Lynch

from

THE OLD BLACK SEA CHEST

Now it was Sally's turn to hang back. Milo kept a tight hold of her hand. He didn't want any tumbles or accidents to spoil this moment. He pulled her with him and they stood looking up at their father, while he smiled down at them.

The smile faded.

'Poor little scraps!' he murmured. 'Thin and shabby, with the look of orphans. It's time their father did come home.'

He sprang from the lorry. Milo stared at him with wondering admiration.

'He's grand!' thought the boy. 'Won't mammy be proud when she sees him!'

'How about the chest, Mr Driscoll?' asked the lorry driver. 'Will I get a lad to bring it up to the house for ye?'

'There's Jim O'Donovan with his barrow!' put in Milo. 'Let him bring it.'

He wanted Jim to share their triumph. Wasn't

he a neighbour?

Timothy Driscoll put some silver into the lorry driver's hand.

'Thanks for your kindness,' he said. 'If you could give me a hand with the chest?'

'Don't bother, we'll fix it! Hi, young Jim! Stand below there and I'll ease it down to you.'

Sally had almost forgotten the black, brass-bound chest. Long ago, a whole year ago, when she was quite small, it had stood in the big room against the wall, the firelight gleaming on its brass nails. It used to hold blankets and winter clothes. Now it shone in the evening sunlight and a crowd to see, wonder, and shout welcomes:

'Hallo, Timothy! Isn't it great you're home again!'

'Ye're looking fine and the old chest is full of diamonds I make no doubt!'

'Welcome back, Tim lad! Glad to see you!'

From all around the voices came, cheering and welcoming.

'Run up, young lad, and tell Mrs Driscoll her man's home!'

Milo and Jim, pushing the hand barrow, led the way. Strangers from the lower town followed the friends and neighbours in a scuffling uneven procession.

'He's terrible grand looking,' whispered Jim. 'I don't suppose ye'll be staying in Bantry. He'll be for shifting yez all to Cork.'

'Where's that child?' demanded the returned wanderer.

He lifted Sally and perched her on the chest, so that she led the triumphal procession. She swayed and slid but managed to stay seated while men and women rushed from shops and houses to shake Timothy Driscoll's hand, to welcome him home and to wonder was the chest filled with gold, diamonds, or just American dollars.

Mrs Driscoll, looking from the open door, saw Sally first, her face white, her eyes blazing, then behind her, Jim and Milo, heads bent as they strained up the hill. And there was Timothy, straight and elegant, his untidy following now joined by the curious idlers of the town.

She meant to go out to the gate to welcome him. But she couldn't, not before all those people. She stepped back, slipped into the chair at the table and burst into tears.

Timothy stopped at the gate and raised his hand.

'Thank you, neighbours,' he said. 'I'll be seeing you all to-morrow!'

He strode into the long low room he had almost forgotten.

'I'm home, Nora!' he said. 'And I'll never go away again.'

He sat beside her and when Milo could no longer

keep Jim and Sally outside with the chest, they
came in and found the two laughing as Timothy
told one of his adventures.

They all helped to bring in the chest and settle
it in its rightful place against the wall. Timothy
Driscoll gave Jim half a crown and shut the door on
him.

'Home at last!' he said, sitting on the chest,
pulling Sally down on one side and Milo at the
other. He tilted back his head at the coloured
parchment map of Ireland in ancient times, which
hung on the wall above.

Milo, too, stared at it. How different it was from
the new shining map beside the big window at
school. He liked this old one best, but he knew the
new map was supposed to be more correct.

'I wonder if it really is,' thought the boy. 'The
man that drew it should know. But how can anyone
be sure?'

'How's my changeling?' asked Timothy Driscoll,
shifting Sally to his knee.

'It is good to see you sitting there!' said Mrs
Driscoll.

Her eyes were happy now, though there were
still tears on her cheeks.

'You must be tired with that long journey from
Cork,' she added.

'That was only the tail of it!' declared Timothy.
'Wait till you hear the whole story.'

Mrs Driscoll stood up.

'Milo! Bring in the tray. Everything's ready and the kettle's boiling.'

Milo whistled when he saw the big tray on the table beside the sink. There was a dish of sliced ham, a salad ready mixed and glowing with slices of tomato. There was soda-bread, cut and buttered, a dish of trifle.

'This is a feast!' declared Timothy. 'I don't deserve it.'

'Won't you open the chest first?' asked Sally in dismay.

Her father and mother looked at one another.

'Sure, the tea's made!' declared Mrs Driscoll. 'You wouldn't want that to be spoiled and your father starving with the hunger!'

So they sat down to the best meal the stay-at-homes had eaten in months.

'I'm glad you're back,' said Sally, talking with her mouth full. 'We haven't had such lovely things to eat since I can remember.'

'Be quiet!' scolded her mother. 'We've had plenty to eat. You wouldn't want ham and salad for your tea every day.'

'I would. I'd love it!' Sally assured her.

They all laughed. But Timothy Driscoll's eyes were very serious.

'I know things must have been very hard here. Yet it wasn't my fault I stayed away so long,' he said. 'I couldn't bear to come back as poor as I went. Now our troubles are over. Besides I did send money home regularly, didn't I? Well, fairly regularly!'

'You did indeed!' agreed his wife, trying not to think of the long gaps when no money, no letter even had come.

'Sure, mammy made lace and people gave her lots of money for that!' declared Sally cheerfully.

'Did you have to go back to that wretched lace-making?' cried Timothy Driscoll. 'Oh, Nora! Why did I ever go away? I should have known!'

'It's lovely lace!' protested Sally. 'One day I'm going to have a black velvet frock and a lace collar to wear on Sundays. One like that!'

She pointed to the almost finished lace collar lying on a sheet of blue tissue-paper in the centre of the window-sill. It was beautiful, with a design of four-leaved shamrocks joined by delicate chains. Only Sally saw its beauty. The others thought of the aching eyes and tired fingers.

'I'll open the chest!' said Timothy.

'We'll finish tea first!' declared his wife.

At last they could eat and drink no more. Sally helped her brother carry out the dirty crocks. She had never seen her mother sit still so long, hands idle on her lap, eyes dreamy, lips smiling.

'You should have come home long ago!' Sally told her father.

'I should indeed have come home sooner,' he muttered.

His fingers shook as he tried to open the chest. The queer thick key had to be turned to the left, then to the right, for this was no ordinary lock. At last he raised the heavy lid and even Mrs Driscoll craned forward to see what was inside.

A shawl of crimson silk lay neatly folded on top. Timothy lifted it out and draped it over her shoulders. Her pale face and dark hair rose from its rich folds so that Sally thought she looked like a queen on her throne. And it was her father who had done this!

'Oh, dadda!' she cried. 'You're great!'

Timothy looked pleased.

'Wait till you see what I've brought you!' he told her.

There was a red and gold chess-board, with chessmen of red and white ivory.

'They must have cost a fortune!' exclaimed Mrs Driscoll. 'And who's going to use them? You're the only one here who can play such clever games!'

'I'll teach Milo,' he said. 'You can watch and decide who wins.'

'That means I'll have to learn too.'

She shook her head doubtfully.

'What time have I for games?'

'When I learn, I'll teach Sally and she'll beat us all!' laughed Milo.

'Am I that clever?' wondered Sally, not at all sure, but longing to play with the elegantly carved red and white pieces.

Next, Timothy brought out a bundle of canvas shoes, worked with red and black flowers, and with yellow straps. The soles were made of thick cord and he held out the smallest pair to Sally.

'Let's see you get into these,' he told her.

She fumbled with the knotted laces of the clumsy boots the cobbler had mended only last week. They were a pair of Milo's he had outgrown and Sally loved tramping around in them, splashing through muddy paths without anyone minding, and kicking stones greater distances than any boys of her own age.

Her father picked one up as she threw it off.

'They're enough to cripple the child!' he complained.

'I can dance in these!' cried Sally, jumping up and unexpectedly sliding the length of the room. She came to a stop against the wall, bumping her chin and knees.

'So you still go round looking as if you were always fighting the Good People!' chuckled Timothy.

'She's one piece of scratches and bruises,' sighed Mrs Driscoll. 'She stumbles into everything and falls over anything possible!'

Sally was too excited over her new shoes to care

what they said. She would wear them at the chapel on Sunday and, afterwards, she'd sit on the wall and swing her legs, so that the people of Bantry, and for miles around, would be able to see her grandeur.

'I am glad you came home,' she told her father, going back to the chest to discover what further wonders were being brought out.

There was a black cabinet, japanned in gold and silver. On the little doors a golden cock with its beak open, gazed steadily at a silver, unknown bird. At the sides were poppies and elegant, slender leaves. Inside were drawers with tiny silver handles and each one was packed with brooches, buckles, rings, bracelets.

As her father pulled out one drawer after another and emptied the contents into his wife's lap, the windows rattled, the old house swayed until Sally thought they must have been transported to the pirate ship in Milo's latest story book.

Timothy picked up a ring of fine filigree gold, with one large pearl. Bending over, he slipped it on his wife's finger. She leaned back, her eyes growing bigger and bigger as she gazed from the lovely ring to the treasures heaped in her lap. She didn't touch them. She seemed almost afraid.

'We're rich!' she whispered. 'I've never seen such wonders!'

She held up her finger and shook her head at the beauty of the pearl ring.

Timothy laughed.

'They're not quite as grand as they look. Mind now, they're not rubbish. They're not too bad at all. But tisn't real diamonds, rubies, emeralds, and pearls you're looking at. They're good paste and, if you had to sell them, you've no need to be ashamed. The gold and silver settings would be worth something. Only, whatever happens, I'd like you to keep the pearl ring. That's real! That's special!'

'Gold and silver, pearls!' echoed Mrs Driscoll. 'And I've been counting pennies. I promise I'll never part with this ring!'

'You'll never have to count pennies again!' declared her husband. 'No more pinching and scraping, no more lace-making. We'll move to Cork and buy a house you'll be proud of. I'll do something where I can use my brains. You'll see!'

'Buy a house!' cried Mrs Driscoll. 'Timothy! Have you all that money?'

'I'll show you!' he said. 'You young ones, out of me way, till I show what I really have brought home!'

He went back to the chest. There were glittering cut-glass tumblers, silver forks and spoons, rolls of silk and velvet, a china tea-set in a wooden box, and a silver teapot.

As Timothy lifted out each marvel, Milo took it from him and placed it on the dresser where the other treasures were ranged, until it was crowded.

'Give me the covered dish, Milo,' said his mother. 'I must put this jewellery safely away.'

The boy handed her the big vegetable dish with the cracked lid and she filled it with the glittering pile in her lap.

Now they all stood around the chest.

'This is for Sally. She'll have music whenever she wants it,' said Timothy Driscoll.

He unwrapped an embroidered tablecloth and showed a polished wooden box with painted figures of a gentleman bowing to a lady on top. A handle stuck out at the side and, as Sally took it, she heard a faint tinkle.

'It's a musical-box!' explained her father. 'Put it away. I can't stand music just now.'

Sally left the tablecloth on the dresser and went slowly upstairs in the dark to her little room with the slip of a window looking out over Bantry.

A faint light shone in from the street lamp higher up the hill and she put the box in the bottom of the cupboard where her best summer frock and her thick coat hung side by side. Then she hurried downstairs.

Her father was standing back from the chest, a puzzled, angry expression on his face.

'What's wrong?' asked Mrs Driscoll, clutching

the crimson shawl closely round her. 'Have you lost something, Timothy? Is it anything of importance?'

He looked round at her, his face suddenly white and strained.

'Anything of importance!' he echoed. 'Oh, not at all! Nothing of importance! Only five thousand pounds!'

Eilís Dillon

from

THE ISLAND OF HORSES

At the far end of the ruined village, just before
the road turned uphill, I had noticed a small,
square, one-roomed building. Its back was to the
west wind, and its three walls were mortared solidly
so that not a chink of light showed inside. Its
fourth side was open. I guessed that it had been a
forge long ago. It had a clean, level, earthen floor,
packed so hard that even in all that time since it
had been used the grass had made poor headway.

'We can easily put a roof on it,' I said. 'There's
furze bushes in plenty up in the fields. The two oars
from the boat will make rafters. We'll be as snug as
if we were at home.'

We each had a strong knife, and a few odd
pieces of string. Up in the high fields, the furze
bushes glowed with deep yellow flowers, the colour
of good butter. It was a joy to breathe in their
sweet, wild scent. We cut branch after branch of
them, and tied them together at their butt ends

with string, so that we could haul them down to the forge. When we had gathered a great pile of them, we went down to the boat for the oars. We carried them up on our shoulders, one each, for they were long and heavy.

Then Pat climbed up on one wall, and I handed him the oars. He laid them across, a few feet apart, and they just reached the opposite wall so that their ends could rest there. We put stones on either end of the oars to weight them down. Then we laid furze branches between them, big ones first, with smaller ones woven through to fill in the gaps. We had to cut a sally stick each from the clump that grew nearby, to poke the branches into place. At last it was finished, and we jumped to the ground and looked at it.

'It's like a huge bird's nest,' I said.

'A bird that would be a bit weak in the head,' said Pat. 'I don't know will it weather a storm. Maybe we should lay big stones on top of the furze, to prevent it from blowing away.'

'And have them come crashing down on top of us in the middle of the night, and we asleep. That roof will hold,' I said confidently. 'At least as long as we'll want it.'

We left a big bundle of branches by the doorway so that we would be able to block it during the night. It had taken a long time to roof the hut and there were still many things to be done. Though the sun was still high, the clouds had begun to turn a faint pink. The wind had got a little colder, too. We were glad that we were to be properly sheltered for the night.

We had to make several journeys up and down from the quay to the hut. We brought some turf, and an old sail, and the whole bag of potatoes. Pat insisted on this, though I thought it would have been enough to have brought up a few, and to have left the bag lying there until the morning. Under the potato bag I found an old blanket that Pat had sneaked from his own home the day before, he said. I knew we were going to be glad of it. I had thought of lying on ferns, and using the old sail as a coverlet, but the ferns would have been full of ticks, all mighty grateful to us for providing them with supper.

When I came up with the last load to the hut, I found that Pat had started a fire with soft, dry turf and furze branches. It smoked a great deal at first, so that I said:

'Anyone seeing that smoke will know that there is someone on the island.'

'I think it's blowing away so quickly that it won't be noticed,' said Pat. 'Anyway we can't prevent it. We must have a fire to roast potatoes.'

Pretty soon there was a little mound of glowing red ashes, and we poked the potatoes into it with our sticks.

'It will be an hour before they're cooked,' I said in despair. 'I can't sit here looking at them. We'll bank them over with turf and go up the road for a while until they're done.'

We broke small pieces of turf, and covered the mound of ashes with them so that they smouldered away finely. Then we each carved a chunk off the soda-loaf, so that we would not die of starvation before the potatoes would be cooked. Munching busily, we set out to follow the road that led uphill across the island.

For the first part it went between stone walls, where fields had been enclosed. There were rabbits everywhere, coming out to play under the slanting evening sun. They were not in the least shy of us, but sat on their haunches wriggling their little noses in that worried way that rabbits do, as they watched us pass. Presently, as the road mounted, the walls disappeared and there was only flat, stony stretches of marshy land on either side. Here sheep would have been grazing comfortably in the old days, but now there was nothing but a couple of moorhens picking their delicate steps from one tussock of sedgy grass to another. The wind sang and whistled up here, much louder than down by the quay. After perhaps half-a-mile, we began to go downhill, and the fields appeared again, more hilly than before. The road took a turn between these hills. As we came around the bend, we both stopped, without a word, to gaze at the scene laid out before us.

This was old Mrs Conroy's silver strand, without a doubt. Now we could see that she was right when she said it was the finest strand in the world. It faced directly out towards the west, with nothing between it and America. This was probably why all the stones had been pounded into fine silver sand. Along the whole length of its glorious curve, the long, slow waves rolled in. We knew that it must be sandy for a long way out, because the waves never broke until they were almost ashore. Then they slid back again with a wonderful, deep singing roar, like a huge organ playing in an empty church. A little above the horizon, the setting sun sent out rays of reddish gold. Little gold-tipped clouds hung over the sea in peaceful groups, as if they were watching us quietly. Slowly and steadily the sun was going down. The sea glowed red, and everything was brighter for a few minutes. Then the wind dropped a little and the song of the waves became louder. All at once, the sun was gone into the sea, and the whole island felt desolate and empty for the first time. Now we saw a big dark cloud spread from the south, as if it had been watching its chance until the sun would be gone. The wind sprang up again and snarled at us meanly. At the same moment, we both found that we wanted to get back to our camp as quickly as possible.

'Up early tomorrow,' said Pat. 'We'll come straight here and go down to that strand. I wish we need never go home.'

'Those people that lived on the island long ago,' I said as we turned and walked back by the way we had come, 'your grandmother's family, and the other families that were here – it must have hurt them sore to leave it. I wonder why they never came back in the summertime, same. I would have, if it was me.'

'She was the only one that wanted to come back,' said Pat. 'She told me that. But she couldn't come back by herself, of course, and none of the others would come with her. She says they suffered so much in that last winter that even years afterwards they used to shiver and turn white at the mention of the Island of Horses.'

I wished he had not told me that. Now I felt that we were being escorted back to the ruined village by an army of ghosts. They were not malignant, but only curious. Still, they gave me the creeps.

'Come along, Pat,' I shouted, 'I'll race you to the camp!'

The ghosts scattered quickly from our flying feet. In a few minutes we were back at the fire, poking the potatoes out from among the ashes. They were perfectly cooked, soft and floury all through. We put more turf on the fire and made it blaze up, rather for company than for its heat, for we were fine and warm after the run. Then we sat at either side of the fire and ate our supper, cutting open the potatoes and digging out their insides with our penknives.

Before we had finished, we had both begun to yawn. We had had an exciting day, but I think we welcomed sleep also because we were beginning to be a little afraid of the solitude of our island. Neither of us said a word about this, but I know that I was mighty glad to be curled up beside Pat in the hut, before the last of the light was gone from the sky. We lay close together on the old sail, covered with the blanket. We had covered the fire with ashes and had filled up the doorway with the remaining branches of furze. There was one big gap between the branches, and presently, through this, I saw a single star. I watched it until I fell asleep.

It was pitch dark when I awoke. The star was gone. I lay very still, hoping that sleep would steal over me again. Then I began to notice what I suppose must have disturbed me. The ground under me seemed to be shaking gently. I listened with every part of me. My very hair seemed to go rigid with a terrible, primitive fear. Over and over my mind kept repeating the words: *The Island of Horses, the Island of Horses*. The shaking of the earth became a sound. There was no mistaking it. It was the sound of hoofbeats on turf. With a cry of fear, I seized Pat's arm and pushed him, rattled him about until he started awake. His voice was easy and sensible.

'Danny, what is it? Don't be afraid.'

'Don't you hear it? It's horses, horses galloping.'

He reached out for my shoulder and held it so that I stopped trembling, while he listened. Then he said softly:

'Yes, horses galloping.'

I felt him twitch the blanket aside. We got up. Still holding my shoulder, he moved towards the doorway. I went with him in a half-dream. The noise was deafening now. Ever so still we stood, hardly breathing, looking out over our barricade of furze. The sky was dark and there was no moon, but a faint greyness might have been the beginning of the dawn. Then past the hut came the horses, thundering along the grassy track. We saw nothing but a mass of flying shadows. Down past the quay they went, and along the island to the south, where we had not yet been. We listened until the sound of their hooves died away. Long after that, we were still listening, thinking that the beating of our own hearts was the drumming of hooves.

At last Pat said, with a little sigh:

'They're gone.'

He dropped his hand from my shoulder. I said uneasily:

'They were real horses.'

'They made enough noise for real horses,' said Pat. 'Tomorrow we'll find them.'

We lay down again, but I could not fall asleep. Each time that I was on the edge of sleep, I would start awake again, imagining that I heard the horses returning. Beside me, Pat lay perfectly still, but I knew by his breathing that he was awake too. At last I heard him give a gentle snore, and I envied him his extra year of life, that made him so cool in the face of such astonishing things.

Presently a grey light began to show up the furze bushes in the doorway. Then the birds began their morning songs. I waited until the sun was up and then I slipped outside, without waking Pat. There had been a frost during the night, and the wind had dropped completely. The sea was a smooth, satiny, pale blue, but with a swell that crashed heavily on the stones beside the quay. All around the hut the grass was cut and torn by the galloping hooves of last night's horses. I was pleased to see it so, for I had still had a little doubt as to whether they had been real.

I poked the hot embers out from among the ashes of last night's fire, and covered them with turf. Then, while I waited for it to blaze up, I went down to the quay to have a look at the boat. It could have been no more than six o'clock. The tide was out a long way, but there was just enough

water at the quay to keep the pookawn afloat. With the way that we had lashed her to the bollards, if she had been left high and dry, she would have been hanging in mid-air now, looking mighty silly. Over to the left, I was surprised to see that there were no rocks, but a great patch of sandy mud uncovered by the tide. As I watched I saw a familiar wriggle on the edge of the sea. I went a little closer to look, and then I raced back to the hut. Pat was sitting up, rubbing his eyes.

'Eels,' I shouted at him. 'Millions of them! Come on!'

He was after me in a flash. He could not believe his eyes when he saw them. They lay in dozens on the surface of the water, floating helplessly. We knew, of course, that congers are quite helpless on a frosty morning, for we had often gone out early after them at home. But neither of us had ever seen so many of them together before.

'We must bring the boat around,' said Pat.

'There's no wind,' I said, 'and the oars are holding up the roof of the house for us.'

''Twould be a sin to let these eels go to waste,' said Pat. 'We'll have to bring the barrels down here to the edge of the water and take them in somehow. If the sun gets a bit warmer, the whole lot of them will get away on us.'

We ran back to the boat. The barrels were big and heavy, made of some kind of hard wood and bound with iron hoops. We had to get a rope round each one, and haul them up out of the boat on to the quay. Then we rolled them along as far as the rocky strand. Getting them over the rocks was a nightmare. Our bare feet were sore and bleeding and our hands raw by the time we had got the two barrels standing at the water's edge.

The eels were still waiting for us. The water was icy cold when we stepped into it, but we had no time to think of that. Old Mrs Conroy's warning that the eels might bite the legs off us was no joke, as we very well knew. Pat had put an old piece of sacking and a short, thick stick into one of the barrels, and these were the whole of our gear. We each took an end of the piece of sacking, holding it wide, and slipped it under one of the milder-looking, middle-sized eels. He glared at us with his big, wicked eyes. We lifted him gently out of the water, and quickly grasped the two ends of the piece of sacking together, so that he was a prisoner. He twitched and jerked, but not much, for he was still cold. Then Pat ran like a redshank with him and tipped him into one of the barrels. He lay on the bottom of it without stirring.

We repeated this many times, until we had almost filled both barrels. We had lids for the barrels, with holes punched in them, and hasps at the sides to hold them in place. These were very necessary, because as soon as there were several eels in the barrels they began to get warm from contact with each other, and to revive. Then they started springing out of the barrels with a strong muscular twitch of their powerful bodies. One whack on the tail with Pat's thick stick made them helpless again. Only one eel escaped us, and we let him go. We said he deserved his luck, but I think the real reason was that his snapping jaws looked so terrifying that we did not fancy tackling him while he was in his full health. He had been the biggest of all.

At last we stood back and stretched ourselves wearily, while we looked with satisfaction at our catch. The sun was well up now, and the eels at the water's edge were submerging one by one, with little quick splashes.

'Just in time,' said Pat. 'Now we must get ropes and moor the barrels to the rocks so that they won't be washed away. We have no hope of getting them into the boat. We'll have to tow them home.'

With the weight of the eels inside them, we were barely able to move the barrels at all. Still, after a lot of hard work, we managed to get them near a big rock that seemed to have its roots buried deeply enough in the sand. We moored them there, with a long rope to each, in the hope that they would float. Then we left them. Getting them in tow with the pookawn would be another day's problem.

Back at the camp, we finished the soda-bread, and drank a great deal of fresh water from the spring well. Then we put potatoes into the hot ashes again for our next meal, and tidied up the hut, for we guessed that we would spend another night there. Pat went to examine the hoof-prints.

'It's hard to say how many horses there were,' he said after a moment. 'They were so much huddled together. I wish we could have seen them. They are not big ones, I'd say.'

Sure enough, the prints looked as if they had been made by Connemara ponies. As we examined them, I thought there was something strange or wrong about them, but I could not discover what it was. An idea had flashed through my mind and was gone again before I could make my own of it.

'It shouldn't be hard to find them, wherever they are,' Pat was saying. 'We'll just follow the tracks. The island is small enough.'

As we went past the head of the quay, we saw that the tide had come in a long way. Over where we had moored them the barrels of eels were already awash. We followed the green path in the opposite direction to that which we had taken last evening. It seemed to run around by the foot of the island. The flying hooves of the horses had made such deep tracks that they were very easy to follow, even when, as happened presently, the path became partly covered in soft sand.

'Now I see what is happening,' I said. 'This is the proper way to the silver strand, that we looked down on last night from the top of the island.'

So it proved to be. About three-quarters of a mile from the camp, we found ourselves at one end of the great, curving strand. Still the path ran along the top, but the tracks of the horses' hooves left it and plunged down across the sand. They spread out a little more now, as if the horses had enjoyed the freedom of the wide space. Still they remained in a group, and we thought we would now be able to guess how many had been there. But this was still impossible.

Strands are always longer than they look. Though the smooth sea never seemed more than a few yards away, we were walking for a long time before we reached it. Still the hoof-prints led us on, outlined clear and hard now in the firm wet sand. Then, all at once, both of us stopped dead. I found my voice first, to say in a half-whisper:

'Pat, those horses galloped into the sea.'

Conor O'Brien

from

THE RUNAWAYS

Above the landing-place there was a rough way up the cliff, partly by narrow natural ledges and partly by steps cut in the rock. Some fifty feet above the sea it widened enough for people to pass when the islanders' boat was drawn up there, as it was for the winter, when all communication was cut off. Above that it got narrower still, and steeper. It would make an unaccustomed head giddy to look down into the water swaying to and fro in the cleft, with plopping and sucking noises echoing up, distinct from the continuous low growling of the surf outside. A hundred feet up, the cliff eased back in a slope of grass and stones, where the path had almost vanished from disuse; the same distance farther up, the shipwrecked party reached a leveller space that showed signs of former cultivation, and beyond it a ruinous house loomed up in the grey dawn. Beet was making slow time up the rough hill-side, wincing as his bare feet trod on a sharp stone or a patch of dwarf furze; the two men had drawn some way ahead, engaged in an incomprehensible argument in Gaelic. At the top of the slope Tom Malachi turned back towards the boys with the substance of it.

'It is what I was saying that we should go up to the old house and see what shelter's in it, for you should be hacked after the night's work. But Con here would have it that we should keep away from the house entirely, for there's a man in it that's in trouble, and the less that knows it the better. That's why he was striving to keep me off the island. Well, I says, I'll go bail you wouldn't inform on him, and you had a right to be inside from the cold. Whoever's in it will have a bit of firing, and that's a thing that's hard to come by on Croaghmore.'

Here was a dilemma for Beet. Only two days out, and he was being thrust into the company of a man who was in trouble, the very thing his father had warned him against. However, the secret was out: Tom Malachi had given away the fact that there was a refugee on the island, and it would not do either party any harm if he was to meet perfect strangers. And he might have a bit of firing; in fact he certainly had, for there was a faint odour of turf- and wood-smoke in the air; and the house had four walls and at least half a roof. All three boys were wet and tired and sleepy, and a chill little wind was sweeping the shelterless hillside. It was silly to risk colds and possible pneumonia by taking Mr Merivale's scruples too literally, so Beet assured Con that they would not inform on anyone.

Con knocked four times on a boarded-up window. After a few moments the glimmer of a candle shone through the chinks between the boards, and he spoke some words of Gaelic into them. The door was opened at once, and a new voice, speaking in English, invited the party inside. It was pleasantly warm and dry there; the blackened rafters still supported mouldering thatch, hardly visible in the light of a single candle, and some sods of turf still glowed on the hearth. Their host knelt down and blew them into a blaze, while Con recounted what had brought the boys there.

'We broke our boat back by the Bullig, and the half of us had to leave her, the way she'd float till she got to Bunassa. The young lads had to swim for it, and I was in dread they might take a cold if I didn't bring them within here.'

'Sure you're welcome, boys,' said the stranger hospitably, though he did not really welcome the invasion. 'Come up to the fire.'

Tom put his hand into a recess beside the fireplace, and sure enough the tinder box was still there. But he could not get the tinder to light; it had become damp after years in an unoccupied house with half the roof off.

'Give me a match, Thady, like a decent lad, the way I'll fire a bush,' he said. 'The old follower will be a long time getting home, and we'd bring out boats quicker if they should see the blaze. We have the world of fish in the seine.'

Privately Thady damned all fishing, but as it was the Bunassa men who provided him with food and shelter he could not well refuse. Anyway, what was done was done, and there was no need for any of the rescue-party to land on the island at all. He handed over the matches, and Tom took them and went out. After he had made his signal he intended to walk across the island and hail the seine-boat for news.

Thady threw an armful of dry heather-roots on to the hearth. They broke into a cheerful blaze. A kettle hanging from a big hook in the chimney began to whimper.

'Strip off your wet clothes, and sit in close to the fire,' he advised the boys. 'One time and I in Canada I saw the Indians making ready to go to bed in an open camp. They'd strip off everything and scorch themselves all round by the fire, and then they'd roll up in their blankets, and they'd be asleep in the turning of a hand. I'll bring the blankets for you.'

The strong firelight now showed Thady Nolan up clearly. Nobody looks at his best when he has spent days in a hovel on an uninhabited island and has been pulled out of bed at three in the morning, but he stood the trying test well. Of course he had a rather disgruntled air. Some lucky men can be 'on the run' for months and yet live comfortably with their friends or relations, but Thady was one of the unlucky. He had found himself in a district where he didn't know a soul except Con Sugrue, and Con had thought it too dangerous to harbour him on the mainland. And the arrangements for getting him off the island were hanging fire.

He was of medium height, getting on for fifty, as a few grey hairs in his dark head showed, but still keeping a clean and athletic figure. He had a seaman's face, with blue eyes surrounded by wrinkles, and a short, pointed beard which he kept carefully trimmed. It was a pleasant, kindly face that looked at the boys as he collected their wet clothes, but a hint of fanatical fire in his eyes suggested that he was just the sort of person who might get into trouble, though not in the ordinary sense a criminal. Beet wondered what sort of trouble he was in. In spite of Mr Merivale's warning he did not really believe in Republican martyrs. Irish affairs had for some years occupied so little space in the English Press that one assumed the conditions in the two countries were the same, and that most of the men in trouble were wanted for crimes of violence or grand larceny; but Thady did not look that sort of man. Foxy, who had more experience of this part of the country, associated island mysteries with contraband or poteen; but Croaghmore was not that sort of island. The uncertainty of landing on it made it useless for that or any other sort of trade.

Con Sugrue, who had sat silent for some time, now spoke.

'I'm thinking, Thady, it would be as well to tell the English boys who you are, the way they wouldn't have all sorts of wrong suspicions.'

Thady assented, though with some hesitation. 'Still,' he told himself, 'the English have queer ideas; maybe they'd think no worse of me if they knew.'

Con did not state the trouble very definitely. 'Thady's a decent, honest man,' he said, 'but he was against the Government, and they have him persecuted out of the globe of Ireland.'

But the word 'persecution' had very different associations for the Merivales. From time to time they had seen appeals in the *Morning Post* on behalf of loyalists who were flying from the persecution of a Government which was neither decent nor honest – though that hardly explained why the refugee should fly to Croaghmore. Con's next words, however, gave a clue to the choice of the island.

'Did you get any sight of the French boat that

should come for you, Thady?'

Anyone who has sailed round this coast knows that most of the craft one sees are Breton lobster-smacks or Spanish trawlers. They are the obvious means of transport for illegal goods.

'I did not,' Thady answered crossly. 'There's not a chance of her, with that damned *Muirchu* up and down every day.'

The *Muirchu* is the Government fishery cruiser. Her job is precisely to keep French smacks away from islands like Croaghmore which are inside the three-mile limit. It looked as if poor Thady was condemned to a long term of imprisonment.

He went back into the room to finish dressing. When he reappeared he was wearing a blue cloth suit, now rather stained and creased, but once a good one, a blue jersey, and a peaked cap. He might have been the mate of a coasting schooner, or even the skipper of a yacht. The hissing and bubbling of the kettle reminded him of his duties as a host. He went to a recess in the wall and took a black bottle out of it.

'You should have something to kill the cold, after the hardship you got,' he said to his visitors. 'I have a drop of rum here, and there's sugar, but there's only the one old mug. You'll have to pass it round.'

The rum punch and the blazing fire were very warming. Soon the boys rolled themselves up in their blankets, and in a moment Beet and Foxy were fast asleep, though their bed was only a pile of heather with a bit of mildewy sail-cloth spread over it. But Pip stayed awake. His brain was seething with a great idea. He sat up and stared at Thady; and the longer he looked, the more he liked him.

'Try another suppeen of the punch,' the refugee suggested. ''Tis a great warrant to put you asleep.'

That wasn't Pip's idea, though he did not refuse the offer. He was thinking how luckily they had been cast up on Croaghmore just now, when the French smack could not get near it. The fishery cruiser could not mistake the *Prion* for one; they were all much larger boats, and they would be easily recognized by the men whose special job it was to look out for them. Why shouldn't the *Prion* do what the Frenchman could not and rescue poor Thady from durance vile? It would be a practical way to repay the night's hospitality. He looked at Thady again. Of course yachting clothes don't make a yachtsman; indeed, on the fronts of popular resorts they generally show just the opposite; but here there was no reason why he should be dressed up as a seaman if he wasn't one. Careful, though; he might be a steamboat-man, and a mere passenger in a sailing yacht, and passengers were too much of a nuisance.

'And are you really a sailor, Mr Nolan?' he asked,

in the tone of one who wants to draw out salty yarns.

'Begor, you may say he is,' Con assured him. 'Thady was brought up in the Capers.'

'The Capers were schooners owned in Cape Clear,' Thady explained, 'and there wasn't a finer school for seamanship that those same vessels, though I say it that shouldn't. I went deep-water, too, an odd time; I was in a small yacht going to South America.'

This sounded more than good enough. A big-ship man might be out of place in the cramped quarters of the little *Prion*, but this man had sailed in a small yacht. Pip wondered how small she was; the last yacht he knew of that had sailed to South America, the one Foxy had been in the year before, was only twenty-five tons, not so much bigger than their own. Thady would surely know how to make himself and them comfortable on board. And an extra hand would be a godsend on the long passage to Skye. Three watch-keepers and a cook make up the right complement for a sea voyage of several days.

'Must you go to France?' he asked eagerly. 'Or would any other country do?'

'Any one would do, so long as I'm out of Ireland.'

'Scotland?'

''Tis all one. I'd surely be able to get a ship in Glasgow.'

Pip jumped up and nearly gave a whoop of joy, but he remembered in time that he did not want to wake the others yet. Beet woke slowly and cantankerously, and he would start raising objections. Pip tried to keep his voice low, in spite of his excitement.

'Then you're coming with us! We've got a yacht, and we're going straight to Scotland, and we're going to keep miles away from the Irish coast. And if anyone sees you, you're our skipper.'

'Bedamn but you're in luck, Thady!' Con exclaimed. 'I seen the yacht in Bunassa yesterday; she's a small thing, but I'd say you'll be a deal better off in her than in the Frenchman, and there's no knowing will she come at all. We'll have the yacht here to-morrow, with the will of God. We'll pay the young gentlemen the same the Frenchman was to get.'

Pip started to protest against the idea of passage-money. If he was doing wrong it seemed more wrong to make a profit out of it. And if the story of the payment came out, they could not keep up the pretence that they had shipped an extra hand in good faith. However, Con, who appeared to be a member of the Committee for evacuating Thady, swore that the payment could never be known.

'Divil a fear of it!' he declared emphatically. 'The money isn't Thady's, but 'tis no concern of

those that gave it how 'tis spent, so that he gets
safe away. Five pounds it was the Frenchman
should get; that's what will be coming to you.'

Five pounds, thought Pip drowsily, as he sat
down again by the fire, would be a nice little
contribution from the Merivales to an expedition
which was being rather too much financed by Foxy.
There was no risk. Thady looked the perfect yacht
skipper, all ready dressed for the part. How he was
to be smuggled aboard might safely be left to the
ingenious Con. They were all too sleepy now to
discuss ways and means.

He heard Con saying, ''Tis as well for us to finish
the punch so,' and the mug was passed round.
'Here's luck to the voyage!' said Pip, and he lay
down and was asleep at once.

Tom Malachi made his signal fire and went to
the top of the island to see what result it had. Away
to the east the follower was making good progress
towards the harbour. Beyond her a trail of smoke
on the hillside above Bunassa answered him. In the
other direction he saw the seine-boat far below him
under the cliffs of Croaghbeg. He had no need to
go down to ask if the fish were still in the net; the
noise of shouting and splashing that came up to
him showed that the marauding monsters were
being kept at bay. Looking eastward again, he saw
the help approaching; three boats were already in
sight, clear-cut against the dawn. It was time to go

down to the house and get ready to meet them.

Thady made a hasty cup of tea and woke the boys. It was broad daylight as they filed down the steep path to the landing-place. What a change from the grim scene of the night before! The swell had gone down as quickly as it had risen, and the tide was at the ebb. The water rose and fell gently against the smooth straight wall of the natural quay, instead of cascading over it. One of the boats backed into it on the top of a sea, and it was easy to jump aboard without soaking again the clothes that had been partly dried before Thady's fire; and the rescue-party had met the follower on their way and were bringing the discarded coats and other garments. Then away round the island, to take the last load of fish.

What the night's catch amounted to the boys did not then know or care. Once alongside the seine-boat, they coiled themselves down on top of the wet net and slept soundly till they were brought alongside their yacht and put aboard her.

THE WRITERS

Marita Conlon-McKenna was born in Dublin and grew up there and in Greystones, Co. Wicklow. She is the author of the internationally acclaimed trilogy of historical novels centring on the Great Famine – *Under the Hawthorn Tree*, *Wildflower Girl* and *Fields of Home* – all of which have been translated into several languages. *Under the Hawthorn Tree* won the International Reading Association Award, the Reading Association of Ireland Award and was shortlisted for the Bisto Book of the Year Award (1990/1); *Wildflower Girl* won the Bisto Historical Fiction Category Award (1991/2). Her other work for children includes the novels *The Blue Horse* (Bisto Book of the Year Award, 1992/3), *No Goodbye* and *Safe Harbour* (shortlisted for the Bisto Book of the Year Award, 1995/6) and a picturebook, *Little Star*. She lives in Co. Dublin with her husband and four children.

Frank Murphy was born in Newcastle West, Co. Limerick. Formerly a primary school teacher and principal, he has written for a wide range of school textbooks in both Irish and English. His first full-length children's novel, *Lockie and Dadge*, won a Bisto Book of the Year Merit Award and the special Eilís Dillon Memorial Award for the author of an outstanding first children's book (1995/6). He has also written *Charlie Harte and His Two-wheeled Tiger* and the text for *Gulliver, a Story Book to Colour*. He currently lives in Cork.

Maeve Friel was born in Derry and educated there and in Dublin. Her first children's book, *The Deerstone*, was shortlisted for the Bisto Book of the Year Award (1992/3), while a later novel, *Distant Voices*, was shortlisted for both the Bisto Book of the Year Award and the Reading Association of Ireland Award (1994/5). Her other novels include *Charlie's Story* and *The Lantern Moon*, the latter of which won a Bisto Book of the Year Merit Award (1996/7). Following a period in which she lived in Britain, she has now returned to Ireland, and lives in Co. Dublin.

Tom McCaughren was born in Ballymena, Co. Antrim, and works as a radio and television journalist with RTE. His five 'fox' stories – *Run with the Wind; Run to Earth; Run Swift, Run Free; Run to the Ark* and *Run to the Wild Wood* – have been translated into various languages and have won several prizes, including the Bisto Book of the Decade 1980/1990 Award for the first three. His other work for children includes an adventure story, *The Silent Sea;* a contemporary Ulster 'troubles' story, *Rainbows of the Moon* and the historical novel *In Search of the Liberty Tree.* He is married, with four grown-up children, and lives in Dublin.

Elizabeth O'Hara is the pen-name of Eilís Ní Dhuibhne, who is a curator at the National Library of Ireland. Under her own name she has written for both adults and children: for children her work includes *Hugo and the Sunshine Girl* and *The Uncommon Cormorant*, the latter shortlisted for the Bisto Book of the Year Award (1990/1). As Elizabeth O'Hara, she has written a trilogy of historical novels: *The*

Hiring Fair (winner of a Bisto Merit Award and the Reading Association of Ireland Book Award 1993/4); *Blaeberry Sunday* (Bisto Book of the Year Award, 1994/5) and *Penny-Farthing Sally*. She lives in Co. Dublin with her husband and family.

Sam McBratney was brought up in Lisburn, Co. Antrim, and educated there and in Dublin. Formerly a teacher at both primary and secondary levels, he is now a full-time writer, producing work for both adults and children. For the latter he has written a wide range of books for an equally wide age-range, including the Jimmy Zest stories and the internationally best-selling picturebook *Guess How Much I Love You*. A novel for teenagers, *Put a Saddle on the Pig*, won a Bisto Merit Award (1992/3), as did his historical story *The Chieftain's Daughter* (1993/4). Among his other titles are *The Green Kids*, *Flash Eddie and the Big Bad Wolf*, *Art, You're Magic!* and *The Lough Neagh Monster*. He is married, with three grown-up children, and lives in Co. Antrim.

Siobhán Parkinson was born in Dublin and educated in Galway, Donegal and Dublin. Two of her books have been shortlisted for Bisto Book of the Year Awards – *Amelia* (1993/4) and *All Shining in the Spring* (1995/6) – while *Sisters ... No Way!* was the outright winner in 1996/7. Her other work for children includes *No Peace for Amelia* and *Four Kids, Three Cats, Two Cows, One Witch (maybe)*. She works in the publishing industry and lives in Dublin with her husband and son.

Matthew Sweeney was born and brought up in Co. Donegal. Since 1973 he has lived in London, broadcasting and talking in schools on the subject of children's reading and writing. In 1994/5 he was Poet in Residence at London's South Bank Centre. As a poet, he has published widely praised collections for both adults and children: his work for the latter comprises *The Flying Spring Onion* and *Fatso in the Red Suit*. His two stories for children are *The Chinese Dressing-Gown* and *The Snow Vulture*. He is married, with two children.

Martin Waddell was born and brought up in Co. Down. Before becoming one of today's most prolific writers of children's books he worked in Britain in printing, publishing and bookselling, in addition to having a short period as apprentice goalkeeper for Fulham. His writing for the young ranges from picturebook texts to teenage fiction. Among the best known of the former are *Can't You Sleep, Little Bear?* (winner of the Smarties Book Prize, 1988); *The Park in the Dark* (winner of the Emil/Kurt Maschler Award, 1989); *Farmer Duck* (winner of the Smarties Book Prize, 1991); *Grandma's Bill* (Bisto Book of the Year Merit Award, 1990/1) and *John Joe and the Big Hen* (shortlisted for the Bisto Book of the Year Award, 1994/5). He has also written the Napper series of football stories and two stories in the Rock River series, featuring Little Obie, his family and friends. His teenage titles include *Tango's Baby* and *The Life and Loves of Zoe T. Curley*. He has also written many novels under the pseudonym Catherine Sefton, including the Ulster trilogy: *The Beat of the Drum*, *Frankie's Story* and *Starry Night*, winner of the Other Award (1986). He is married, with three grown-up children, and lives in Co. Down.

John Quinn was born in Co. Meath and worked as a primary teacher before becoming a radio producer with RTE, where a number of his documentary programmes have won prestigious awards. He has written one adult novel and four for children: *The Summer of Lily and Esme* (winner of the Bisto Book of the Year Award, 1991/2, and shortlisted for the Reading Association of Ireland Award, 1993), *The Gold Cross of Killadoo*, *Duck and Swan* and *One Fine Day*. He is married, with a grown-up family, and lives in Co. Galway.

Eugene McCabe was born in Glasgow but has lived for many years in Co. Monaghan. He is highly regarded as a playwright, for both stage and television, his plays including *King of the Castle, Swift* and the television trilogy *Victims*. His prose works include *Heritage and Other Stories*, *Death and Nightingales* and his one children's book, *Cyril: The Quest of an Orphaned Squirrel*, winner of the 1987 Reading Association of Ireland Book Award.

Janet McNeill (1907-1994) was born in Dublin and educated in England and Scotland. On her return to Ireland, she worked as a journalist in Belfast and wrote various short stories, novels and opera librettos for adults. For children, she wrote radio plays, a series of short stories featuring the schoolboy Specs McCann and his friends, and a number of novels, including *The Battle of St George Without; Goodbye, Dove Square; Tom's Tower; We Three*

★ 187 ★

Kings and *The Prisoner in the Park*. The last years of her life were spent in Bristol.

Meta Mayne Reid (1905-1991) was born in Yorkshire of Irish parents and educated there and in Manchester. From 1930 onwards, most of her life was spent in Ulster, which, particularly Co. Down and Co. Derry, was to be the setting for most of her children's novels. These fall into two principal categories: historical fiction (such as *The Silver Fighting Cocks*, *The Two Rebels* and *Beyond the Wide World's End*) and stories with a contemporary setting, often with a basis in fantasy (such as *The McNeills at Rathcapple*, *With Angus in the Forest* and *The Glen Beyond the Door*). Her last years were spent in Co. Down.

Walter Macken (1915-1967) was born in Galway and educated there. Much of his life was devoted to the theatre, both in Ireland and outside, for which, in addition to acting, he wrote and directed a wide range of plays. He wrote a number of novels and short stories for adults and two works of fiction for children: *Island of the Great Yellow Ox* and *The Flight of the Doves*. He died in Co. Galway.

Patricia Lynch (1898-1972) was born in Cork and educated in Ireland, Britain and Belgium. She was the author of over fifty children's novels, many of which were translated into almost every European language. The most widely known of her stories are those featuring the Turf-Cutter's donkey and those featuring Brogeen. Other titles include *The Grey Goose of Kilnevin*, *Fiddler's Quest*, *The Mad O'Haras*, *The Dark Sailor of Youghal*, *The*

Bookshop on the Quay, *The Old Black Sea Chest* and *Back of Beyond*. Many of these have been reissued in recent years. She spent her last years in Dublin.

Eilís Dillon (1920-1994) was born in Galway and educated there and in Sligo. Abandoning a career as a professional cellist, she turned to writing for adults and children, quickly earning an international reputation for both. Among her numerous children's books are *The Lost Island*, *The San Sebastian*, *The Singing Cave*, *The Coriander*, *The Cruise of the Santa Maria*, *The Five Hundred*, *The Island of Horses* (included in a *Sunday Times* listing of the hundred best books of all time for children) and *The Island of Ghosts*, winner of the Bisto Book of the Year Award, 1990/1. For a number of years she divided her time between Ireland, Italy and America, before returning to Dublin, where she died.

Conor O'Brien (1880-1952) was born in Co. Limerick and educated in Ireland and England. By profession an architect, he was an expert mountaineer and yachtsman: he was the first Irishman to sail around the world in his own yacht, *Saoirse*, a journey which took precisely two years (June 1923-1925). For adults he wrote a series of books on sailing, including an account of his voyage on *Saoirse*. For younger readers he wrote a number of boys' adventure stories, including *Two Boys Go Sailing*, *The Runaways*, *The Castaways* and *The Luck of the Golden Salmon*. After many travels and periods of residence abroad, he returned to Ireland, where he died in Foynes, Co. Limerick.

SOURCES

FIELDS OF HOME, Marita Conlon-McKenna: published by The O'Brien Press Ltd., Dublin, and in the USA (hardback edition) by Holiday House Inc., New York; reproduced with permission.

LOCKIE AND DADGE, Frank Murphy: published by The O'Brien Press Ltd., Dublin.

DISTANT VOICES, Maeve Friel: published by Poolbeg Press Ltd., Dublin; reproduced with permission.

IN SEARCH OF THE LIBERTY TREE, Tom McCaughren: published by The Children's Press Ltd., Dublin; reproduced with permission.

THE HIRING FAIR, Elizabeth O'Hara: published by Poolbeg Press Ltd., Dublin; reproduced with permission.

THE CHIEFTAIN'S DAUGHTER, Sam McBratney: published by The O'Brien Press Ltd., Dublin.

AMELIA, Siobhán Parkinson: published by The O'Brien Press Ltd., Dublin.

THE SNOW VULTURE, Matthew Sweeney: published by Faber and Faber Ltd., London; reproduced with permission.

LITTLE OBIE AND THE FLOOD, Martin Waddell, illustrated by Elsie Lennox. Reproduced with permission of the publisher, Walker Books Ltd., London.

THE SUMMER OF LILY AND ESME, John Quinn: published by Poolbeg Press Ltd., Dublin; reproduced with permission.

CYRIL: THE QUEST OF AN ORPHANED SQUIRREL, Eugene McCabe: published by The O'Brien Press Ltd, Dublin.

WE THREE KINGS, Janet McNeill; reproduced with permission of AP Watt Ltd. on behalf of David Alexander.

THE TWO REBELS, Meta Mayne Reid; reproduced with permission of Dr Mark Reid.

THE FLIGHT OF THE DOVES, Walter Macken: published by Macmillan Children's Books Ltd., London; reproduced with permission of the publisher and the estate of Walter Macken.

THE OLD BLACK SEA CHEST, Patricia Lynch; reproduced with permission of Eugene Lambert and the Patricia Lynch estate.

THE ISLAND OF HORSES, Eilís Dillon; published by Faber and Faber Ltd., London; reproduced with permission of the publishers.

THE RUNAWAYS, Conor O'Brien; reproduced with permission of the Conor O'Brien estate.